the secret life of Samantha McGregor
BOOK ONE

bad
connection

a novel

---

melody carlson

Multnomah ® Publishers

BAD CONNECTION

published by Multnomah Publishers *A division of Random House, Inc.* and in association with the literary agency of Sara A. Fortenberry

© 2006 by Carlson Management Co., Inc.

International Standard Book Number: 1-59052-692-9

Cover design by Studiogearbox.com

Cover photo by Steve Gardner, www.shootpw.com

Unless otherwise indicated, Scripture quotations are from:

The Message © 1993, 1994, 1995, 1996, 2000, 2001, 2002

Used by permission of NavPress Publishing Group

Other Scripture quotations are from:

The Holy Bible, King James Version (KJV)

Multnomah is a trademark of Multnomah Publishers and is registered in the U.S. Patent and Trademark Office. The colophon is a trademark of Multnomah Publishers.

Printed in the United States of America

LIBRARY OF CONGRESS CATALOGING-IN-PUBLICATION DATA

Carlson, Melody.

Bad connection : a novel / Melody Carlson.

    p. cm. — (The secret life of Samantha McGregor ; bk. 1)

ISBN 1-59052-692-9

    1. Teenage girls—Fiction. 2. Missing persons—Fiction. 3. Teenagers—Psychic ability—Fiction. I. Title. II. Series: Carlson, Melody. Secret life of Samantha McGregor ; bk. 1.

PS3553.A73257B35 2006

813'.54—dc22

2006013162

For information:
MULTNOMAH PUBLISHERS, INC.
12265 ORACLE BOULEVARD, SUITE 200
COLORADO SPRINGS, CO 80921

06 07 08 09 10—10 9 8 7 6 5 4 3 2 1

Author s Note

I normally don't include a letter in my books, but because The Secret Life of Samantha McGregor series treads on some new territory, I want to make some things as clear as possible. First of all, this book is *fiction*—it's simply a story that's meant to entertain and to possibly point out some spiritual truths—it is *not* a theological study on the proper use of the gifts of the Holy Spirit. While I do believe in the gifts of the Holy Spirit and that God wants all of us to do many wonderful things, I also realize that Samantha's gift, her ability to receive dreams and visions from God, is extremely rare and unique—but it does make for a good story!

Second, my hope is that you won't envy Samantha's unusual gift or seek it for yourself, since that would be totally wrong! Don't forget that God is the giver of every good and perfect gift and *He's* the One who decides who gets what and when it's appropriate to use. If you go around searching for your own gifts, you can put yourself at serious risk. Satan masquerades himself as an angel of light and delights in tricking those who look for gifts in the wrong places. Don't let that be you.

More than anything, I hope that you'll follow Samantha's example by seeking out God and a committed relationship with Him. I hope that you'll desire to walk closely with God every day, to make Him your best friend, and be ready for whatever adventures and gifts He has in store for you. Just make sure they come from God!

And finally, remember that the Bible is our ultimate source for all of life's questions. That's why I've included more Scripture in this series than usual. Also, please check out the resources and discussion questions in the back of this book.

I pray that this fictional journey will draw your heart closer to God and that He will be your lifeline—for today and for always!

Best blessings!

Melody Carlson

A Word from Samantha

The first time it happened, I thought it was pretty weird but kind of cool. The second time it happened, I got a little freaked. The third time it happened, I became seriously scared and had sort of a meltdown. That's when my mom decided to send me to a shrink. She thought I was going crazy. And I thought she was right for a change.

Turns out it was just God. Okay, not just God. Because, believe me, God is way more than just anything. Still, it was hard to explain this weird phenomenon to my mom or the shrink or anyone. It still is. Other than my best friend, Olivia, I don't think most people really get me.

But that's okay, because I know that God gets me. For that reason, I try to keep this part of my life under wraps. For the most part anyway.

One

The wipers slap furiously, whipping back and forth like wild things, but the windshield remains a murky puddle before my eyes. I lean forward and push my chest against the steering wheel as I try to see what's ahead. The curving road is pitch-black—dark and shiny—and the blindingly bright headlights of the vehicle tailgating me don't help.

Why did I take this road? And why am I driving so late at night? I adjust my rearview mirror to subdue the lights, and then I step on the gas in an attempt to outrun the impatient jerk. Or maybe I should just pull over. But where?

Just when I think I've lost my tailgater, a truck barrels down the road toward me, its lights glaring straight into my already compromised vision. The wimpy wipers don't help at all, and I can barely see as I start to brake because it looks like the truck has crossed the centerline into my lane. It feels like he's hurtling straight toward me—a head-on about to happen!

I jerk the steering wheel to the right and swerve off the road, hitting the gravel shoulder at about fifty miles an hour and totally out of control. Then in the same split second, certain that my car is about to dive into the steep ditch and roll, I crank my steering wheel back to the left and careen across both lanes of the highway, crashing straight through the end of the guardrail, almost as if it's not even there.

There's this moment of eerie silence as my car, free of gravity, plunges into thin air and total darkness. But when it lands, it's like an explosion. And the jolt to my body is shocking then numbing. I can't breathe. It feels as if someone has a pillow over my face, and my chest and head ache from the impact. Something cold and wet creeps up my legs like the fingers of death. I try to kick whatever it is away, but my legs are pinned to the seat, unable to move.

I free my arms in an attempt to fight off this thing that's suffocating me, but it seems to deflate just as quickly as it came—the airbag. I peer through my shattered windshield. My left headlight illuminates what appears to be water running swiftly all around me. And I remember, yes, the Willamette River runs along this stretch of country road.

My car's not fully submerged in the river yet, although the front end is partially in the water. But I feel the car shift, as if the wheels aren't on solid ground. I force the gear into reverse, hoping that I can back up, but the movement makes the car lurch forward. I prepare myself to be swallowed by the river. Stuck in this car, my death trap. How long does it take a vehicle to sink? How long does it take to drown?

A new rush of adrenaline hits me. I'm not ready to give up. I push the button for the electric windows, but they don't budge. I attempt to force open the door, but it's stuck tight. Even if I got it open, I can't free my legs from whatever pins them down.

The water's up to my waist now and numbingly cold. Or have I lost all feeling in the lower half of my body? I'm not sure if it's the dashboard pressed down against my thighs. Or maybe it's the engine. I don't know. But I know that I'm trapped.

It seems almost silly, but it's as if time stands still, and I begin to analyze how I got to this place. I made a bad decision tonight. I didn't have to take this road. But don't we all make bad decisions sometimes? Why this? Why me? Why now?

I look up and catch my reflection in the cockeyed rearview mirror. But it's not my face I see. I blink then stare back into the mirror. *Who is this woman staring back at me?* At first she seems old, maybe fortysomething, and then she seems young, like my age.

Finally I realize that it's not me at all—it's my friend Kayla Henderson. Her blond hair is pulled back in a ponytail, and her dark brown eyes are full of fear with tears streaming down her cheeks. An image of pure terror and desperation.

And that's when I wake up.

My heart still pounds frantically as I sit up in my bed and look around, making sure that I'm still in my own room, safe and warm and dry. I wiggle my toes. Just fine. Nothing to be afraid of. It was only a dream…just a dream. But an *unusual* dream. What does it mean?

I glance at the clock. It's 5:31 and too early to get up. But going back to sleep seems unlikely too. So I turn on the light by my bed and, out of habit, reach for my Bible, opening it to a very familiar section marked with a red ribbon.

Oh, I know these words already. My dad was the first one to read this portion of Scripture to me, back when I had my first *unusual* dream. And it was Dad who encouraged me to memorize this Scripture as well as others. "Write them in your heart," he'd said. My dad seemed to be the one person who really got me back then, back when this whole thing seemed to start up. But it comforted me to know that he seemed to understand and even respect what he called my "gift."

So I read this Scripture now, hearing the words almost as if Dad were here right beside me, quietly whispering them to me.

> And ye shall know that I am in the midst of Israel, and that I am the LORD your God, and none else: and my people shall never be ashamed. And it shall come to pass afterward, that I will pour out my spirit upon all flesh; and your sons and your daughters shall prophesy, your old men shall dream dreams, your young men shall see visions: And also upon the servants and upon the handmaids in those days will I pour out my spirit. (Joel 2:27–29, KJV)

"That's exactly what God is doing in you, Samantha," Dad told me the first time I proudly recited this Scripture.

"What do you mean?" I asked, although I felt fairly sure that I knew.

"God's pouring out His Spirit on you. Giving you visions and dreams."

"But why? Why did God pick *me*?"

Dad just smiled. "He must've known that you have the right kind of heart, honey. And He designed you in such a way that you could handle something of this magnitude. Just trust Him."

I close my Bible as well as my eyes, trying to remember the details of the dream that just interrupted my sleep. Why does it seem unusual? Was it supposed to mean something? Some kind of message? Was it really from God?

I get out of bed and walk back and forth in my room, running over the events of the dream, trying to sort it out, to discern whether it's something to be dismissed or something I should pay attention to. I mean, sometimes I have dreams that are simply dreams. Other times…well, those are different.

Obviously my dream involved a car wreck. It was nighttime, and the car went into the Willamette River. And it seemed like Kayla Henderson was involved. Is it possible that Kayla was driving? That she's been involved in a real accident? That could explain why she's been missing these past few days. Maybe her car is sitting on the bottom of the river right now. Or maybe I'm just blowing this all out of proportion. Sometimes I wonder why God can't just get a loudspeaker or a TV series or a big billboard that would grab everyone's attention and just make Himself perfectly clear.

Yet even as I try to make light of this, the chilling thought of poor Kayla being the victim of a horrible accident, sitting pinned in a car at the bottom of a river, sends a serious shiver down my spine. I pull on my sweatshirt, stick my feet into my UGGs, and go out to the kitchen, where I turn on the lights and start to make a pot of coffee.

My mom always appreciates it when I do this, not that I do it too often, but I nearly drop the glass coffee carafe when I hear the deep sound of a man's voice talking behind me. I almost think that it's God. But I turn to see that it's only the TV.

Sometimes when my mom's feeling extra stressed, she'll set it to turn on at six in the morning. She calls it her "gentle" alarm clock. Although the tone of this dude's voice feels anything but gentle. Still, he's got my attention, and I stand there holding the half-filled coffee carafe as I listen.

"Breaking news near Fremont early this morning," he says in an urgent voice. *"Forty-six-year-old Cindy James lost control of her Nissan on wet roads, crashing through the guardrail and plummeting thirty feet into the Willamette River shortly before midnight last night. The accident occurred just five miles south of Fremont. Fortunately for Ms. James, two other drivers witnessed the wreck and immediately called 911. Gary Forsythe of Gresham and Hank Burns of eastern Washington scaled the steep river-bank to see the car partially submerged in the turbulent waters. Swift-thinking Burns then managed to return to his truck to get a chain and a rope, which the two men were able to secure to a nearby tree and her bumper, prevent-ing the small car from being completely submerged and swept away by the current."*

As he describes the wreck, some footage is being shown, and it seems very similar to how it was in my dream. Although the perspective is different. And there's another thing. Instead of Kayla Henderson in the driver's seat, it seems it was this Cindy James person. They show a photo of someone I've never seen before. Or maybe it's the person I got a glimpse of just before I saw Kayla.

But now I question whether I really did see Kayla. Maybe I just imagined it was her because I've felt so concerned about her these past couple of days. Or maybe I just got a bad connection. I'm not sure. But I guess I'm relieved that it's not my friend in the wreck. And I'm relieved that Cindy James seems to be doing okay too.

"Ms. James suffered a broken collar bone and several fractured ribs, but after emergency crews used the Jaws of Life to extract her from the crushed car, she was transported to Fremont General Hospital and is said to be in good condition."

I stand there for a few more minutes as they hit other news highlights that don't mean much to me, and they finally move on to the weather outlook for the rest of the week. But as I continue making coffee, I have to wonder why I had that dream. I mean, it seems that Cindy James's situation was under control. It's not like she needed my help. And it obviously had nothing to do with Kayla. So I gotta wonder, why would God use my "gift" to disrupt a perfectly good night's sleep with something that really has nothing to do with me? I don't get it.

I suppose I'm sort of distracted by all this as I plod through my morning routines—getting dressed, eating some breakfast, riding to school with my best friend, Olivia. But it's not until we're on our way to PE, which is fourth period and right before lunch, that Olivia confronts me.

"You seem kinda moody today. Everything okay, Sam?"

"Yeah." I shrug, trying to brush it off. No reason to burden her with my little problem, which isn't really a problem. It's more like an irritation.

But then after PE, as we're all getting dressed in the locker room, the conversation, once again, becomes focused on Kayla Henderson. She's been the hot topic among the girls for the past few days—everyone seems to be speculating on where she is right now. And naturally, especially after this morning's dream, I am easily pulled in.

"Everyone *knows* that Kayla is a tramp," says Emma Piscolli in a very superior-sounding voice.

"That's a little harsh," I say as I button my jeans.

"She's slept with half the guys in school," continues Emma.

In moments like this, it's hard to believe that Emma actually used to be one of Kayla's best friends. But then there was that big fight over Parker Davis last spring. I guess love triangles leave everyone wounded.

"You know this for a fact, Emma?" demands Olivia. "Do you have a tracking device or a monitor on her or something?"

I try to laugh, hoping it might lighten things up. "Yeah, and if you do, can you tell us where she's at right now?"

"Or who she's with?" adds Brittany Fallows.

Emma pulls her T-shirt over her head then puts both hands on her hips. "I can make a pretty good guess."

"What?" asks Brittany.

"I think Kayla has run off to get married."

Naturally, this makes us all laugh.

"I'm *not* kidding."

"Yeah, right." Olivia rolls her eyes. "Like who gets married while they're still in high school? Tell us another one, Emma."

"I'm serious." Emma looks at me now. "Don't you remember that guy Kayla told us about not that long ago? The one she met last summer?"

"Oh yeah," I say as I recall about a month back when Kayla and Emma and I worked to set up the photo exhibit for the Fall Art Fair. "She did tell us about this really cool guy she met while she was visiting her aunt in San Diego. Saying how great looking he was and how he was really into her." Okay, I don't admit that I hadn't totally believed Kayla at the time, how I thought maybe she was making the whole thing up for Emma's benefit since I suspected she was still hurting over the breakup with Parker Davis.

Emma nods. "And I happen to know she'd been e-mailing this guy regularly."

"An online romance?" asks Brittany.

"Yeah." Emma picks up her bag and slings a strap over her shoulder. "And I think that's where Kayla is right now."

"Okay, even if Kayla was having an online romance, what makes you think she'd want to get married?" I ask in a slightly cynical tone. "That's so totally ridiculous."

"Yeah," says Olivia. "It's crazy, Emma."

"How many girls do you know who get married at our age?" I point out as I zip my boot.

"Not unless they're insane or rednecks..." says Brittany.

"Or pregnant." Emma's brows arch with suspicion.

"An online pregnancy," says Olivia. "Now that's a new one for the medical journals."

"I didn't *say* she was pregnant," retorts Emma.

"No," I toss back at her. "Just that she's getting married."

"Hey, it's just a guess."

"A *stupid* guess." Olivia looks at me. "Ready to go to lunch, Sam?"

We tell the others good-bye and head out of the stuffy locker room.

"Can you believe Emma?" Olivia says as we head down the hall toward the cafeteria. "I know Kayla has her problems..." Olivia sighs. "And I guess it's true that she's gotten a little wild this past year. But running away to get married? It seems pretty far-fetched to me."

"Yeah, it's hard to believe." But as we get in the lunch line, I'm thinking that it's also hard to believe how much Kayla has changed since middle school, back when we were still good friends and Kayla was more into soccer than guys. But we all grow up and change. Even so, it makes me sad. And I'm still trying to figure out why she made that sudden appearance in my dream. Is God trying to tell me something?

"Do you think anything really happened to her?" Olivia glances at me as she fills her cup with ice.

I shrug as I pick up a drink cup. I tell Olivia a lot of things, but I'm just not ready to tell her about this. Not that I have anything to tell. Not really.

"I mean, have you gotten any feelings about her?" she asks in a hushed tone, I'm sure so that no one will hear.

Olivia knows about the few "unusual experiences" I've had in the past. Although, up until this morning, I haven't had anything happen to me for almost a year now. I actually hoped that it was all over. That God had moved on, picked someone else… I guess I was wrong.

"Not really," I say lightly. "Not anything that means anything. Of course, I'm worried about her, and I've been praying for her. But that's pretty much where it ends." Okay, I'd probably say more, but there are too many listening ears right now.

"It's just so weird. I really thought she'd be back by now."

"How long has she been gone?" I ask.

"Well, I heard her mom on the news last night. She hadn't seen Kayla since Saturday. And it's Wednesday today."

"It really doesn't sound good." I pick up a tuna sandwich and set it on my tray. "And I know things aren't too cool at her house—they haven't been for the past couple of years, ever since her parents split up. I guess I just figured maybe Kayla ran away to stay at a friend's house, you know, to just lay low for a while. Maybe she thought it would get her mom's attention."

"What friend though?"

"I know…"

"Well, it has gotten her mom's attention. Did you see the news last night? She was really crying and falling apart."

I shake my head. "I missed that."

"It's just so weird."

"Yeah. Pretty weird." Okay, that's an understatement. The truth is, I can't think of Kayla today without feeling seriously worried.

Where is she?

TWO

Olivia and I pay the cashier and go find an empty table, where we sit down and, as usual, bow our heads. We don't pray out loud. But we do pray. And sometimes we take some heat over our lunch blessing.

Some people call us religious freaks, and one guy likes to call us "the nuns." But we just laugh it off. No big deal. It might be harder if we had to handle it alone. Having a best friend by your side makes a lot of things easier. I thank God for Olivia on a daily basis.

"So, if she's not at a friend's house…" continues Olivia, obviously still stuck on the Kayla mystery. "Where do you think she is, Sam? Do you think she's been kidnapped?"

"Not according to the news the other day." I stick a straw in my drink.

"I know. They say she took her purse and clothes and money and stuff and that it looked like it was clearly a run-away situation. Her mom told the news that she hadn't been home all day on Saturday. But isn't it possible that someone entered the house and forced Kayla to get those things, tried to make it look normal?"

I kind of laugh. "Can you imagine a kidnapper breaking into your house and then telling you to neatly pack your bags?"

"I guess that sounds kind of nutty."

Just then we are joined by Emma and Brittany and a couple of other girls. And although we haven't been that close with these girls during the past year or so, I'm not that surprised they've been hanging with us lately. I know it has to do with our old connection to Kayla. It's like we're all worried and slightly freaked, and something about being together and talking about it seems to help some of them. Maybe it's therapeutic.

Though to be honest, it makes me uncomfortable. Especially today. And some of the speculations, particularly this latest one from Emma, who never seemed all that concerned about Kayla in the first place, can be rather maddening.

"Did you guys hear Emma's latest theory?" Amelia Carnes asks as she sits next to me. "About why Kayla is missing?"

"You mean her little marriage hypothesis?" I venture.

Amelia laughs. "Yeah, is that nuts or what?"

"I think she just *hopes* it's true." Brittany jabs Emma with her elbow as they sit across from us. "That way she won't have to keep competing with Kayla for the attention of Parker Davis."

"Yeah, right. Everyone knows that Parker and I are history now anyway."

"That's for sure." Amelia nods over to a nearby table where Parker is obviously flirting with Corrine Ashton.

"I couldn't care less," retorts Emma. "I'm totally over him."

"He seems to be totally over you too," observes Olivia.

"It's mutual." Emma blows the wrapper off her straw, right in Olivia's face.

"So that doesn't have anything to do with your story about Kayla running off to get married?" I ask.

"Nothing whatsoever."

"But why are you so sure of this now, Emma?" asks Amelia. "You never mentioned it to anyone before."

"I was at her house last night. Her mom let me get on her computer, and I was reading some old e-mails."

"No way!" Brittany leans forward. Actually, I think we're all leaning forward now. "She wrote about it in her e-mails?"

"Was there really any talk of marriage?" I ask.

"Well, these were old e-mails," Emma admits. "We're guessing she may have deleted the more recent ones, to erase the trail, you know. But judging by the old e-mails, we could tell that this guy was really into her."

"What's his name?" I ask.

"His first name is Colby. But we couldn't find his last name anywhere."

"Do the police know about this?"

Emma nods. "Yeah, Kayla's mom has let them go through her room and their whole house. They downloaded every-thing from her computer and took some other things too."

"Still," I persist, "I don't get why you think that Kayla would run off to marry this Colby kid. I mean, how would they even support themselves? Get real! What kind of life could two teenagers possibly have down in San Diego? Slinging hamburgers at McDonald's and living out of their car or maybe on a beach?"

"Yeah," says Amelia. "Even if Kayla was that desperate, she's not that stupid."

Emma nods and smiles, and I get this feeling that she's holding something back. Like a poker player who's got a couple of aces, she's waiting for the right moment to lay down her hand.

"Okay," I say to Emma. "What is it? What do you know that you're not telling us?"

"Yeah," says Brittany. "And don't tell us Kayla got pregnant online either."

We kind of laugh again. But I can tell the laughter is getting thinner and weaker. Maybe humor worked for us on Monday, when we all just assumed that Kayla had pulled a fast one. And even on Tuesday, when we figured she was holding out to punish her mom over this latest boyfriend. But now that it's Wednesday, well, I think we're all getting pretty worried.

"Okay, this is the deal," Emma says as if she's divulging a big secret. "This Colby guy is in his twenties. He's not our age at all."

Everyone looks properly shocked, and it's obvious that Emma is pleased. I suspect she's enjoying all this attention. No wonder she keeps dragging it out.

But now that I think about it, I remember something like this. "Yeah, I kind of recall Kayla saying the guy she met was older, but I assumed it was just like a year or two. Are you sure he's really that old, Emma?"

"Well, according to the e-mail I read, he's a graduate of UCLA, and he has a good job and a nice apartment and a cool car and everything."

"That's just weird," I say. "Why would a guy like that be interested in someone like Kayla?" Okay, even as I say this, I realize it could be taken all wrong. Still, it doesn't make sense.

"Kayla's a pretty girl," offers Brittany. "And you gotta admit she looks great in a bikini. Didn't you say that they met on a beach, Emma?"

"Yep. That's what she told me."

"She said that to me too," I admit. "Seems like he was a surfer."

"Kayla went on and on about what a great time they'd had at the beach," says Emma.

"Even so," I say, "if this Colby dude really is a college grad with a good job and everything, well, why would he get involved with a minor? There are laws against that, you know."

Olivia shakes her head. "It really doesn't make much sense."

"Maybe Kayla told him she was older," suggests Emma. "I mean, she could easily pass for twenty-one. Don't you think? Any of us could."

"Yeah." Brittany points at Emma. "And some of us even have the fake ID to prove it."

"Shut *up!*" Emma shoots back.

Brittany just laughs. "But it's true; Kayla could pass for being older."

"Still, why would she go down there now?" I ask. "It's less than a month until winter break. She could've gone then."

"She was obviously desperate to see him," says Emma. "Remember she said he was hot? Maybe she was worried that some other chick was going to turn his head and steal his affections." She laughs.

"Yeah," Brittany says in a sarcastic tone. "Wonder where she'd ever get an idea like that, *Emma*?"

"Hey, I went out with Parker before Kayla did."

"One date does not count as *going out* with a guy, Emma," says Amelia.

"But I really liked him."

"Whatever!" Olivia shakes her head, and I can tell she's losing patience. "Back to Kayla now."

"That's right," I say. "Back to Kayla. Seriously, Emma, do you really think she went down there to *marry* this Colby guy?"

Emma smiles, perhaps a little too smugly. "I think so. And furthermore, so does Kayla's very own mother."

"But on the news last night," Olivia reminds her, "her mom was so broken up. She was falling apart."

"Duh." Emma nods. "It's not like she's going to tell the whole world that her sixteen–year-old daughter ran off to marry a man in his twenties. Ya think?"

"Maybe not…" I frown as I consider this. "But something still doesn't quite ring true."

Olivia gives me a curious look. "What do you think, Sam?"

I kind of shrug. "I don't know, but it just seems a little freaky that this Colby guy… I mean, this grown man who supposedly has it all together is seriously interested in Kayla, wanting to marry her? Even if she was pretending to be older, it still doesn't make sense. Surely he could tell that she was, well, you know, kind of immature."

"Ya'd think," agrees Amelia.

"Unless he's really a nerd," suggests Olivia. "Kayla might've exaggerated his good looks."

"I wonder if there are any photos." I glance at Emma.

"Nope. The police already searched everywhere. Nothing like that was found."

"I don't buy that," says Amelia. "Why would Kayla be so eager to run down there and marry this guy if he really was a nerd? Kayla is definitely not into nerd-types."

"Good point." Brittany nods.

"Okay, maybe it's just a hunch," Emma says, "but I remember this time when Kayla and I were talking—back before the thing with Parker happened—and Kayla was saying how much she hated living at home. And you guys know how weird her mom's been since her dad left. Anyway, Kayla told me that the first chance she had to leave, she'd be outta there. She even told me how she would imagine Prince Charming coming to take her away. And yeah, it seemed silly at the time, but looking back… I think that's just what she was looking for."

"And you think she found her Prince Charming in Colby?" Olivia asks.

Emma nods. "And that's what I told the police."

"Did they buy it?" I ask.

She shrugs. "I think they're looking into it."

"Have they called her aunt in San Diego?"

"Of course, Samantha." But Emma just shakes her head. "She hasn't heard a word from her."

"Yeah," I admit. "I guess that wouldn't be too smart. I mean, if she really does want to get married and not be found."

"So is that it?" asks Olivia. "We just figure Kayla has married Colby and that they'll live happily ever after?"

Amelia laughs. "Yeah, right. What are the odds of a marriage with a sixteen-year-old and a UCLA grad making it?"

"Maybe if it's just about the sex?" Emma suggests with a devious twinkle in her eye.

"You *would* say that," says Brittany.

"Well, I think it's very sad." Olivia frowns.

I nod. "I think it's tragic."

"You mean the part about the sex?" teases Emma.

I shrug. "Whatever."

"Okay, here comes the sweet little Christian lecture about how we should all be saving ourselves for our future husbands." Emma looks directly at Olivia and me.

I glance at my watch. "Don't worry," I say as I stand and pick up my tray. "There's no time for a sermon right now, but if you'd like to schedule something for, say—"

"No, no. That's okay." Emma winks at me.

"Thanks for enlightening us about Kayla," Olivia tells Emma. "I think..."

"I personally don't know what to think," Brittany admits as we walk over to dump our trays.

"Yeah." Amelia nods. "It's pretty bizarre."

As I walk toward the science department, I'm thinking about the "sermon" that I'd really like to give Emma. I'd like to explain that the reason God wants her to save sex for marriage is only because He loves her so much that He wants her to have the best life possible. I'd like to say the same things my dad said to me back when I had just turned twelve. Of course, it had seemed a little premature at the time, but then not long after our little talk, he was gone.

Three

My first unusual dream involved a guinea pig and my dad. Oh, my dad wasn't in the dream, but he helped me to resolve it. I was about six at the time, and I had this vivid dream where I was actually the lost brown and white rodent.

The next morning, I explained to my dad how I'd been stuck in this cement tunnel-like thing. At first he didn't take me too seriously, but when I couldn't let it go and went on and on with detailed descriptions of how it felt to be trapped and how it was cold and damp and scary and how I knew that it was Porky—my neighbor's missing guinea pig—who was really trapped in the tunnel-like thing, Dad actually started to listen.

Suddenly he remembered some new houses that were going up on the street behind us, and he'd seen a truck just a few days before bringing in some of those "tunnel-like" things—he told me they were called culverts.

So he and I walked over to the site, and he explained the situation. I'm sure the construction guys never would've taken me seriously, but Dad, ready for his shift, was wearing his police uniform, and maybe the workers actually thought he was doing an official investigation.

Whatever the case, we went straight over to the one culvert that had been partially installed, and Dad talked them into moving some rocks and stuff. And there, trapped inside the cement tube, was Porky, the lost guinea pig.

"You got ESP or something?" one of the guys asked me as I cuddled the shivering guinea pig up to my chest.

"ES what?"

Dad just laughed. "It's a gift," he told them. I had a few more dreams after that, not terribly dramatic, but when they turned out to be true, my dad took notice.

I was about twelve, not long after my Dad gave me his little sex talk, when I experienced another unusual dream. I didn't really understand it at the time, but I could tell it meant something.

I'm not unlike other people in that I have lots of dreams. And as far as I know, lots of my dreams don't mean a thing. They're just plain old dreams. Learning to differentiate between what is purely my brain entertaining itself while I'm catching z's and something that's meant to be a message from God hasn't been easy. In fact, I still don't have it totally figured out.

But the dream that caught my attention that time was about my dad. It wasn't exactly a bad dream, but I did wake up feeling extremely sad. I think I was actually crying. Although I wasn't even sure why. I mean, the dream really wasn't that big of a deal. Or so I assumed at the time. I suppose I just brushed it off as nothing.

In that dream, Dad and I had been walking together along the top of this big stone wall. At first I'd been holding

his hand because I was afraid I was going to fall. The wall
was so tall and steep that I couldn't even see the ground
below us, just mist. But after a bit I started to relax.

It was fun hopping along from rock to rock, and I
must've let go of his hand. And maybe I'd been talking
or just not paying attention, but after a while I looked up
and realized that my dad and I were no longer walking
together. We were walking on two separate walls, about
fifty feet apart, and between these walls stretched this
huge gulf of just nothingness.

My dad waved to me from where he was walking on the
other side, and he seemed perfectly fine. But I was confused and scared and couldn't figure out how I would get
over there to join him. Not only that, but the more we
walked, the farther apart the two walls became. There
seemed no way to get back to him, and I woke up totally
frustrated. But thinking it was just a weird dream, I never
told anyone about it. Just mulled it over myself and then
sort of forgot it.

Until three days later, when my dad was killed while on
duty, shot by some creep who got caught cooking meth in
his basement. Dad died instantly, and we never got a
chance to say good-bye or I love you or anything.

The minute I heard the news, I remembered my
dream. That's when I knew that it had been a warning. But
I also knew that I had failed to heed it. I had failed my own
father—the only person who really understood my gift, the
only person who really got me. Consequently, I was
drowning in guilt. And I was mad at God.

During the next couple of years, I didn't completely turn my back on God, but I was so hurt and confused that I tried to ignore Him. I also never wanted to experience that "gift" again. The "gift," I had decided by that time, was actually a curse in disguise. Something to be avoided at all costs. I wanted no part of it.

For the first time in my life, I felt very much alone. I deeply missed my dad, and I was pushing away my heavenly Father too. And as a result, I was totally miserable. My whole family was suffering over the loss of Dad. My older brother, Zach, started getting into trouble, and I began to get into ridiculous fights with my mom. And not unlike Porky the guinea pig, I felt trapped in this cold, dark hole that only seemed to get deeper. There seemed no way out, and it was lonely down there.

Finally I got tired of my depressed isolation. And as much as I missed my dad, I began to miss God even more. I had just turned fifteen, and it was the summer before our sophomore year, and somehow Olivia talked me into going on a youth group retreat with her. I hadn't been involved with youth group for a couple of years by then, and Mom had long since given up trying to get me to go. Her hands were already full with her job at the park district, plus Zach and his problems. I'd pretty much been doing as I liked. Which wasn't anything exciting.

Anyway, I reluctantly went with Olivia to the retreat, and after several days of stoiclike resistance to the programs and messages, God got to me. God got to me in a very big way, and I knew that I'd been a fool to think I could avoid Him. More than that, I knew that I'd never ever leave Him again. And it was shortly after that retreat that I experienced the gift again. But this time I was wide awake. It wasn't a dream. It was a vision.

It's hard to describe what it was like. I mean, my eyes were wide open, and I was just sitting out in the back-yard, in the old tree house Dad and Zach had built ages ago, actually praying, when it happened. Suddenly I saw something unreal—like something that was lit up. But it wasn't like watching a movie exactly. It was more like this flash, like an image I saw in my mind as much as it seemed like I saw it with my eyes. And I suspect it hap-pened really fast.

At first I thought I was having a stroke or an aneurysm since it was kind of like a burst of light inside my brain. But as I focused and concentrated, trying to recall what I'd actually seen, I got this strong sensation of peace. And I knew what I'd experienced was a God-thing. And as weird as it sounds, it's like I got this sneak peek into heaven, and I know that it was my dad standing there in front of me, and I know that he was happy. As simple as that, and yet it was so incredibly strong and vivid and real. Amazingly cool. And right there, sitting in the musty old tree house, I lifted my hands and praised God.

Okay, I figured it was probably just a one-time thing. And that was just peachy with me. I never even made the connection that it might have to do with my old "gift" of dreaming dreams. I just figured it was God's way of assur-ing me that things were okay with Dad, and that there were no hard feelings against me for not telling him about the walking on the wall dream.

I decided to tell Mom about it, and although she said "That's nice," I could tell she thought it was pretty weird. And even though I told her it was a God-thing and that it wasn't scary or anything, she seemed uncomfortable. It occurred to me that she hadn't really been going to church much since Dad's death, and I realized how I hardly ever heard her talk about God anymore. And it hit me that she had changed. We all had.

About six months later I had another vision episode. And once again, it caught me totally off guard. It was during Christmas break last year, and Mom had talked me into helping out at the park district's day care center to earn a little extra money. It was afternoon recess, and as usual, I was out on the playground supervising the kids along with a couple of the teachers when I experienced a flash very similar to the one in the tree house. I'm sure it was just a split-second thing, but in that moment it seemed longer as I envisioned three-year-old Aaron Giles tumbling from the top of the slide, toppling over the handrail, and plunging headfirst to the ground.

Without even thinking, I started running straight for the slide, and just as I got there it happened. Somehow—only with God's help—I caught the little guy in midair, knocking us both to the ground. But I took most of the impact, which left a nice purple bruise on my rear end for a while. The little boy looked as astonished as I felt sitting there in the sawdust with him sprawled across my lap.

"Oh–my–gosh!" exclaimed Kellie, one of the senior teachers, as she raced over to join us. "I saw the whole thing! Is he okay?"

Aaron blinked up at Kellie and nodded. Then Kellie helped us both to our feet. "How about you, Samantha? Are you okay?"

"Seem to be."

"How on earth did you see *that* coming?" she asked with wide eyes.

"I think it was a God-thing," I told her.

"Wow." And although Kellie is this kind of tie-dyed, earth muffin, politically correct, liberal type, she just slowly nodded. "That's cool."

I smiled at her, but as I walked away my knees started to shake. And that's when the enormity of what could've just happened began to hit me full force. What if I hadn't trusted that vision? What if I had hesitated?

Soon all the teachers were talking about Samantha McGregor's amazing rescue. And I suppose I was sort of the hero of the day. And yet the pressure of thinking about how it might've all gone wrong and how guilty I would've felt if Aaron had been injured or even killed was making me a basket case. And by the time Mom and I were in the car after work, I felt like a bundle of raw nerves.

She'd already heard most of the story from the rest of the staff, but as she drove us home, I tried to explain about the vision part and how it kind of scared me. I could tell it was making her uneasy, and she didn't really have any answers for me. But it was pretty disturbing when she suggested that maybe I should see a counselor.

"Why?"

"I think you need to deal with your grief about losing Dad."

"Me?" I thought that I was actually handling it better than both she and Zach combined.

"Yes, Samantha. You seem to be overspiritualizing some things. I think it's a way of compensating, but I'm worried that it might not be healthy."

I wasn't sure what to think about that. But before I went to bed that night, as I prayed, I told God that I didn't really think I was up for this. I told Him that the idea of having these visions was too scary, that I was too young, and that I'd really appreciate it if He'd give this special gift to someone else—someone more responsible, more mature, more worthy.

That was almost a year ago. Almost a year and about six rather uneventful counseling sessions with a shrink-friend of my mom's. And so far so good. Nothing out of the ordinary has happened to me since the thing with Aaron falling off the slide. And I'm thinking, cool, I can live with that. Nothing wrong with being ordinary...normal...

But as I sit here in biology class today, running these old thoughts through my head, I can't help but notice the seat where Kayla would be sitting, if she were here that is. I try to wrap my head around the freaky idea that she is down in sunny San Diego tying the knot with some UCLA grad named Colby. But it's just too weird. So I decide to pray for her.

Dear God, please bring this girl back to her senses. Show her that she needs to return home and that she needs to finish high school, and most of all show her that she needs to invite You back into her life—the sooner the better. Amen.

Kayla actually used to be a Christian. Ironically enough, she was a strong believer back when I was really struggling with my own faith during middle school. But then she got into high school and got distracted with boys. She even admitted to me not long ago that she had fallen away. Still, she's always fairly open to talk about God, and she never puts me down for being a Christian.

So I'm sitting here in this dimly lit room, trying to pay attention to the boring DNA video that Mr. Brant is playing for the class, but I'm distracted by Kayla's empty chair. Hard to miss since it's directly in front of me.

And then totally without warning, I get that exploding flash of light in my head. And instead of seeing the chain of colorful chromosomes on the screen, I see Kayla hunched down in what seems to be the backseat of a car, and she's crying. That's all. Then it's over, and all I see is that crooked chain of chromosomes again—as if only a second or two has passed.

I lean back in my chair and close my eyes, taking in a deep breath. Was that real? Was it from God? And if so, what am I supposed to do about it? What *can* I do? I mean, all I saw was the image of Kayla in a car, crying. What does that mean?

But now the lights are turned on fully, and Mr. Brant is telling us to get out our notebooks and prepare for a quick quiz about what we've just seen. And I'm thinking, really? He's going to ask me about Kayla in the backseat of a car? Like what model was the car? What color? Then I realize, no, this is about DNA. And as I prepare myself to fail this quiz, I wonder why God would give me such a sketchy vision about Kayla and why during biology when I should be focusing on learning something instead.

As soon as class is over, I have this really strong urge to tell Olivia about the vision. Like I think maybe that will take care of it. Olivia can scratch her head, tell me I'm crazy, and then I can move on. No big deal. Only chances are, Olivia will believe the whole thing, and then she'll want me to figure it out. But how can I? Especially when I'm not even certain that it really did come from God?

I mean, there I was thinking about and praying for Kayla, and then there was this weird video playing. Isn't it just possible I imagined the whole thing? But even as I say this to myself, I know that's not the case.

Still, I remember how worried Olivia seems to be about Kayla, how she's sort of obsessing over it, imagining the worst, and I just don't think it's right for me to dump on her yet. How can I tell her that I just saw Kayla and that she was miserable and crying in the backseat of a car? A *blue* car!

Just then it hits me that the interior of the car was gray, and the strip I could see outside the window was a metallic blue. I actually jot this down in my notebook. Not that it means anything exactly. But it might. Then I hurry on to U.S. history. But as I go, I pray. I ask God to confirm if what I saw in biology was really from Him, and if so, I ask Him to show me what to do next. *Help me, God,* I silently plead as I push open the door to class, *I'm in over my head and I need Your direction. Amen.*

Four

My last class of the day is drama. I'm still not even sure why I took it, except that I needed an elective, and last August during registration Olivia talked me into it. "We'll take it together," she told me. "It'll be fun."

Of course, what Olivia didn't know then was that her schedule would change when she got promoted to advanced choir, which is only offered during seventh period. So here I am, stuck in drama without her.

Lately our class has been meeting in the auditorium, where we're slowly working our way through Shakespeare's *Hamlet*. Lucky me, I got the part of Queen Gertrude, the twisted wife of the evil king who murdered his brother, Hamlet's father. Lovely.

"Hey, Samantha," says Kendall Zilcowski, as she slips into the seat next to mine. Besides Kayla, who is still obviously missing, Kendall is the closest thing I have to a friend in this class. And while we're not exactly close, she does manage to make me feel less alone.

"Hey, Kendall." I smile at her. "What's up?"

"Did you hear the latest about Kayla?" she whispers as Mr. Owens walks up the stairs to the stage.

Now, I'm unsure what "the latest" actually means or

why Kendall would know it. But then, I remind myself, it did seem like Kendall and Kayla were getting to be fairly good friends, especially following the fated love triangle that drove a wedge between Emma and Kayla. Maybe Kendall does know something. "Has Kayla shown up?" I ask hopefully. "Is she okay?"

"I haven't heard that she's back home or anything like that. But I did hear that she was reported to have been seen getting on a bus Saturday afternoon."

I frown. "Headed to San Diego?"

"I guess."

Now Mr. Owens clears his throat, our cue that he's about to begin his introduction to today's scene. I open my script to where we left off yesterday, then turn my attention back to Kendall.

"So she left of her own free will?" I whisper and Kendall nods.

Mr. Owens begins to speak. Using his deep theatrical voice, he reminds us of where we've been so far in *Hamlet*…Denmark…the gloomy castle…the king's murder… "And today we'll pick it up in act 4, scene 5. We're at Elsinore, in a room in the castle. Prepare to enter: Queen Gertrude, Horatio, and a Gentleman. Ophelia and King Claudius, you're on deck." He pauses to look down at where we're still sitting in the front rows of the auditorium. "I assume Kayla Henderson is absent again today?"

"She is," answers Kendall.

"Then Kendall, you will continue taking her place as Ophelia please."

"Okay."

"Get in your places, players." He claps his hands in that way that makes everyone think he's gay, although we know he has a wife.

We start scuttling up the stairs to the stage. I should be thankful that we don't have to memorize these lines. Especially since the archaic words feel more like Greek than English to me. I mean, I go over them, and I do think about the story, but sometimes I just don't get it. Like today. Even though I've read through this particular line of Queen Gertrude's a couple of times and it sort of made sense, I still feel lost. It's part of a conversation with Ophelia. And suddenly it's my turn to deliver it.

"To my sick soul," I begin to read in my best dramatic voice, since I don't want Mr. Owens to make me do it again. "As sin's true nature is, each toy seems prologue to some great amiss: So full of artless jealousy is guilt, it spills itself in fearing to be spilt."

The next few minutes is an exchange between Queen Gertrude and Ophelia, with Kendall doing a pretty good job of playing the poor, fated Ophelia, who will later drown herself. Fortunately, these shorter lines seem to make a bit more sense, and it's obvious that Gertrude is uncomfortable, probably feeling guilty. And it's also clear that Ophelia is starting to act a little nutty, probably because of all she's been through. Then King Claudius, played by Simon Valencia, begins his lines, talking to Ophelia, and I'm just standing by, still on stage, just watching and listening.

But Ophelia's lines just keep getting crazier and crazier, and as hard as I try to make sense of them, I just
don't get it. Then just as Ophelia is delivering this little
poem piece, kind of singing it, I suddenly experience that
flash of light again, just like in biology. But instead of seeing Kendall, with her pixielike face and her short dark hair,
I suddenly see Kayla's smooth features, her shoulder-
length straight blond hair, and her big brown eyes brim-
ming with tears. And instead of Kendall's voice, I hear
Kayla's, and it's full of emotion. I blink hard and force
myself to listen carefully.

"Young men will do't, if they come to't; by cock, they
are to blame. Quoth she, 'Before you tumbled me, you
promis'd me to wed.' He answers, 'So would I ha' done,
by yonder sun, An thou hadst not come to my bed.'"

Then just as quickly as it happened, all returns to normal.
Kendall is still here and Kayla is nowhere to be seen.
But it's like I can still feel Kayla's presence up here on the
stage, almost as if she's looking over my shoulder. Very
weird. Fortunately, my lines are pretty minimal after that.
And before long we're done and class ends, and without
even talking to Kendall, I hurry out of the auditorium, heading straight for the bathroom.

I feel kind of sick inside as I actually throw some cold
water onto my face and take in a long, deep breath. Then I
go into a stall for privacy, closing the door and leaning
against it. I take out my script again, going back to the place
where I saw Kayla's face when Kendall was reading
Ophelia's lines. I reread the words slowly, pausing at the part

that says, "You tumbled me, you promis'd me to wed. So would I ha' done, by yonder sun, An thou hadst not come to my bed." That was part of the same section where I felt that I saw and heard Kayla reading. But what does it mean?

Once again, I pray. I ask God if He's actually trying to show me something. I mean, it really does seem like it. I guess I'm just worried that I'm not fully getting it. It just doesn't seem totally clear. So I pull out my Bible and just open it. I do this sometimes when I'm not sure about something and don't know where to look for guidance. And while I'm not saying it's the best way to get answers, I'm often surprised at how easily God can talk to me through His Word—even randomly like this. And this is what I read today.

> "My people were lost sheep. Their shepherds led them astray. They abandoned them in the mountains where they wandered aimless through the hills. They lost track of home, couldn't remember where they came from. Everyone who met them took advantage of them. Their enemies had no qualms: 'Fair game' they said. 'They walked out on GOD. They abandoned the True Pasture, the hope of their parents.'" (Jeremiah 50:6-7)

I read this section a couple more times, and then I thank God. *I know You're showing me something. I know that You want to use me to help Kayla, but I'm not exactly sure what to do. Please, lead me.*

"Samantha?" calls a voice that sounds like Olivia.

"Yeah." I emerge from the bathroom stall and force a wimpy smile.

"Are you okay?"

I nod as I stuff my Bible back into my backpack.

"I was looking all over for you, and Kendall said she saw you come in here. She said you didn't look too well after drama class. You're not sick, are you? You look kind of pale."

"I'm okay. Just some weird stuff going on. I needed a quiet place…to think about some things and to clear my head…and to pray."

"Looks like you found it in here." She glances around the vacant restroom then back at me. "What kind of weird stuff do you mean, Sam?"

"How about if I tell you on the way home?"

As we go to the locker bay, I silently pray some more. I ask God whether or not I should tell Olivia about what I've experienced this afternoon. I mean, as badly as I want to unload all of this onto someone in an earth suit, first I want to be sure that it's the right thing to do. Olivia already feels really bad about Kayla's disappearance. I don't want to involve her without God's approval.

Then we're out in her car, and I'm still grappling with what to do. As she drives away from school, Olivia breaks the ice. "Look, Sam, I know something's up."

"Huh?"

"About Kayla. I was really praying for her last night, and I just got this strong feeling that God is going to show you something about her. Has He revealed anything yet?"

"Seriously?" I turn and study my best friend. "*You* got a feeling?"

"Yeah. But that was all it was. Just a feeling. It's not like I *saw* anything. But because of that feeling I've really been praying for you, Sam. And I understand how you feel about all this stuff. I mean, I remember how hard it was for you last year when you went to the shrink and everything. And I know how you believed that you weren't going to have any more dreams or visions. But I just keep getting this very strong sense…that God is going to use you somehow."

She sighs. "Or maybe it's just hopeful thinking on my part." Olivia turns and looks at me as she waits at the red stoplight. "Maybe it's just because I'm seriously worried about Kayla. I think she's in trouble."

Now, besides my mom and her shrink-friend, who really didn't believe me anyway, Olivia's the only person who I've told any of this stuff to. And she's heard almost all of it—the dreams and visions and everything. And while I know she doesn't totally understand it (and neither do I), she's very understanding about it, and like my dad, she seems to respect that it's from God.

As the stoplight turns green, I believe that God is giving me a green light as well, so I open up to her. First, I tell her about this morning's dream and how it seemed resolved— well, other than seeing Kayla in it. Then I tell her about the vision of Kayla crying in the backseat of a car during biology.

"But we were watching this weird DNA video," I point out, almost as a disclaimer. "And I was looking at Kayla's empty chair and probably remembering my dream...and, well, maybe I just imagined it."

"You don't really believe that, do you?"

"No..."

"So was that it then? Just the dream about the wreck and then the vision of Kayla in the car? I mean, not that those things aren't big. Or not enough. But I guess I'm just not sure where you'd go from there."

"I know." So then I tell her about Shakespeare and *Hamlet* and Ophelia played by Kendall then surprisingly overridden by Kayla—at least for me. "It's like I really saw her standing right there, and I heard her reading Kendall's lines like it was really from her heart. And she had tears in her eyes."

"Freaky!"

"Tell me about it." I quickly open my backpack and pull out the script. "You want to hear the lines?"

"Sure."

So I read the lines again. And this time they seem to make even more sense than before. "You see, Ophelia is talking about betrayal," I explain. "She says 'before you tumbled me'—meaning like you tricked me—but she's saying that before he promised to marry her. And it would've been 'done by yonder sun,' like it would've been done yesterday, but he never showed up. Isn't that weird?"

"Wow..."

"I know...*wow*."

"So, do you think this Colby guy promised to marry Kayla and then changed his mind?"

I shrug. "Maybe..."

"Then wouldn't she come back home?"

"You'd think."

"But I wonder why she was crying in the backseat of a car?" muses Olivia. "I mean, why the backseat? Why not the front seat?"

"I don't know."

"Do you think she's in some kind of real trouble?"

"I'm not sure, but there's another thing..."

"What? No holding out on me, Sam."

"Okay. But for now let's just keep all this stuff between us, all right? I don't want anyone thinking I'm going off the deep end again. Especially my mom. She's got enough on her plate with Zach right now."

"But I thought he was doing better. Isn't he still working at the video store?"

"Yeah, but I guess he's missed a couple of days, and he's been late coming home again. Not a good sign."

"No..." Olivia sighs. "I'm sorry, Sam."

"Yeah. Me too. I just hope he's staying clean and sober."

"Well, I pray for him every day."

"Me too. If only prayers alone could change people."

"But back to Kayla, you said there was something else. Another vision?"

"No. More like a confirmation." I reach into my pack for my Bible, opening it to the place I marked with a scrap of notebook paper. "In the bathroom, I was feeling pretty freaked, so I asked God to help me to figure this thing out, to show me whether it was really from Him, you know? And I did the random thing, just opened the Bible up, and this was the first Scripture I laid my eyes on." I read it to her.

"Wow!" She just shakes her head. "That is amazing. Do you think Kayla has been led astray? Or abandoned in the mountains?"

"Yeah, like there's a lot of mountains in San Diego."

"It might be metaphorical," suggests Olivia.

"But even though she's left home, I doubt that she would've forgotten where she came from already. It's only been a few days."

"Unless she has amnesia." Olivia says this in a dramatic voice.

"I think that's just something they do in soap operas. I don't think real people get amnesia that much."

"Well, it looks like God is confirming this thing, Sam. I think He's definitely trying to tell you something."

"I know. I just wish I had a better idea of what exactly it is so I could actually do something... Well, besides pray that is."

"Do you think you should tell her mom?"

"I'm not sure. I've been thinking about it. But I don't really know Mrs. Henderson that well. And I could end up sounding like a nutcase."

"What about the police?"

"I've been thinking about that too. But I'm worried about the same thing there. I mean, how do I go in and tell a policeman that I saw Kayla playing Ophelia in drama today, but she wasn't really there? Even if I got him to believe me, what does it all mean?"

"But what about the car? Did you see a license plate? Or could you tell what make it was?"

"Just a metallic blue. With gray interior."

"Well, that sure narrows it down." Olivia kind of laughs.

"But what about my dream this morning? It was pretty right-on because that woman, Cindy James, really did have a wreck just like in my dream. But I don't get why Kayla was in the dream too. That makes no sense."

"Maybe God just wanted to get your attention," she says thoughtfully. "Maybe He wanted you to see that your dream really was on target so that you'd trust Him."

"I don't know…"

"And maybe He put Kayla into that dream so you'd be thinking of her, so you'd know that she needs help too."

"I suppose that could be."

"Remember, God really does work in mysterious ways, Sam."

"You can say that again." But now I'm obsessing over the Ophelia lines, those words about promising to marry and then being jilted, and it feels like it's a big clue. But if Colby decided not to get married, which makes perfect sense now that I know more about him, then why wouldn't Kayla be back home by now? I run these thoughts past Olivia, and she just shakes her head.

"Man, it seems like the more you know, the murkier it gets."

"That's just what I was thinking." I sigh and look out the window.

"But you do know this, Sam."

"What?"

"God wants you on the case. He's trying to show you something. You need to stay tuned in."

I kind of laugh now. "Right, *stay tuned in*. Like I was going to tune God out."

"You know what I mean."

"I guess. But I have to admit that it's making me uncomfortable. I really thought the whole vision and dream thing was over and done with. It had been nearly a year, Olivia."

"But *I* had a feeling." She smiles as she reminds me. "I got a really strong sense that it wasn't over."

"So why doesn't God show *you* these things instead of me? Why can't you be the one to have visions and dreams and all this crazy stuff?"

"You'd have to ask God that one," she says as she pulls up at my house.

"Thanks a lot," I tell her without enthusiasm. "Maybe I will."

"I'd invite myself in, but I have a mountain of homework, and I need to practice my flute solo for the winter concert. Plus it's midweek service tonight. Need a ride?"

"Sure."

"But before you go in, I want to tell you about this Scripture I read in 1 Corinthians 12 last night. It reminded me of you because it talks about the different spiritual gifts the Holy Spirit gives us and how God works in our lives in

different ways. It's really cool. To one person He gives
the gift of special knowledge, to someone else He gives
the power to heal the sick, and to another the ability to
prophesy. But the Holy Spirit is the only One who distributes
these gifts."

I nod. "Yeah, okay…"

"God is the One who decides who gets what, Sam."

"Thanks." I smile at her.

"See ya."

I go into the house, trying to feel encouraged by the
Scripture she just told me about, but as I drop my backpack on my bed, I still have to ask God, "Why *am* I so
special? Why are You letting *me* in on all these things?
What is it about me?"

I stare at my rather ordinary reflection in the mirror
above my dresser, taking in my curly brown shoulder-
length hair and hazel eyes, those few stubborn freckles,
and the somber expression Zach used to tease me about,
bugging me about why I was always so serious. And all I
can think is that I look like such a kid. Even if I am going
on seventeen in January, I sometimes think I could pass
for twelve or thirteen. And I almost laugh.

"Seriously, God, You must be pretty hard up for help to
call on someone as insignificant as me." Then I feel bad
for sounding ungrateful or even unwilling. So I add, "Even
so, You know that I want to do Your will. And as long as
You're the one doing the leading, I promise to follow."

I just hope I don't end up looking like a total fool.

Five

I had almost expected God to show me something new about Kayla at the midweek service tonight, but while the worship was good and the sermon encouraging, I experienced no visions, and since I didn't fall asleep, no dreams—nothing out of the ordinary.

Naturally, Olivia questions me on this during the drive home.

"Nada," I tell her. "And I was really trying to listen too."

"Maybe you shouldn't try so hard. I mean, you were never trying during those other times, were you?"

I nod. "Yeah, you're right. They just seemed to happen."

"Maybe God needs you to be more relaxed."

"Maybe." I let out a deep sigh and lean back. "But it's a heavy load, Olivia. If God really is trying to tell me something about Kayla, like if she's in danger or something…well, it seems like a lot to expect of a person…like me."

"God must believe you're up to it."

"But don't you think it's kind of weird?"

"Of course it's weird, Sam. Visions, dreams…it must be pretty spooky sometimes. I'm not sure I could handle it myself."

"I don't mean weird like that." I'm trying to think of a way to describe what's bugging me right now, but I feel stuck.

"What then?"

"Well, remember last year, when I was going to that shrink-friend of Mom's? I keep thinking about the time when she pointed out that some Christians might think some of my experiences are kind of New Agey. Like I'm claiming to be some kind of a Christian clairvoyant. She even pointed out how some people might actually assume that I'm demonized or working in cahoots with the devil, you know what I mean?"

"Yeah, I remember you told me about that and how it bothered you."

"I mean, it's pretty hard to describe this kind of thing or what it really means—I guess it even makes me nervous. I'm sure that's why I never talk to anyone about it."

"You talk to me about it, Samantha."

"And I thank God for you, Olivia. I honestly think I'd be going crazy if I had to keep this all to myself—especially today."

"So anyway, you're worried that something's wrong here? Like if you really are a psychic, how could you be a Christian too?

"Bingo!" I nod. "It's like an oxymoron—a *Christian psychic*. Who would believe it?"

"But see, that's where I think some Christians short-change God. It's like they want to put Him in this tiny little box. How can anyone say that God can't gift people in whatever way He chooses? He's God, isn't He? And not to put you on their level, but what about the old prophets in the

Bible? Wouldn't some people call them New Age or even religious psychics today? Wouldn't they be ostracized for their ability to predict the future even if it was God-given?"

"Maybe so…" I kind of laugh. "Come to think of it, a lot of them weren't treated too well during their own time."

"Exactly. And that's only because we humans don't usually know what God is up to."

"And even if God tries to let us in on things, sometimes we question it anyway."

"Well, I believe that God has lots and lots of gifts to give His kids," she persists. "Including things like prophecy and dreaming dreams and having visions. But maybe some of us are just too busy to notice."

"Maybe…"

"Or maybe you're just special, Samantha."

I roll my eyes. "Yeah, maybe…"

"Just know that I'm here for you," she says as she pulls in front of my house. "I'm praying for you, and you can talk to me about any of this. And I won't tell anyone about it either."

"Thanks."

I can tell by Zach's old beater car in the driveway that my wayward brother must've decided to come home before midnight for a change. I say a quick prayer as I go into the house. Zach hasn't exactly been easy to get along with lately, and I'm guessing my mom is still at the park district board meeting.

My brother is sacked out on the couch in the family room as an obnoxious action movie is blaring from the TV.

Zach's coat and backpack and shoes and junk, along with the remnants of what looks like the entire contents of our refrigerator, are spewed all over the room like a hurricane just swept through.

"Zach?" I whisper. But no answer. I turn off the TV, thinking the silence might rouse him, but he's just lying there. I actually go over to look more closely, worried that something might really be wrong, but it appears that he's just totally conked out. I hope it's just plain tiredness, but I know that it could be something more.

I put a throw blanket over him, gather up some of his mess, and take it into the kitchen. It's not like I want to be an enabler exactly, but at the same time, I don't enjoy the idea of Mom walking in and seeing him like this. She has enough stress.

On my way to my room, I pause in the stairway to look at a family photo that was taken when I was eleven. It was my first trip to Disneyland and our last family vacation. The four of us are standing in front of the entrance together— we're all smiling, looking forward to a fun day of rides and adventure. Zach was about fourteen, and although he was starting to act like an obnoxious teenager, things were still going fairly smoothly for us as a family. And as I recall, it was a really fun trip. As I study this photo, I think that for all practical purposes, we just look like your average all-American family. Not perfect, of course, but relatively happy. Like life is good, and it can only get better…

A lump grows in my throat as I consider how much things have changed since that photo was taken. Within that year, Dad was killed. Then Mom pretty much turned into a workaholic, struggling to make ends meet. Later on Zach got involved with alcohol and drugs and has been in and out of rehab twice this past year. And here I am thinking God's sending me messages, which I know some people would equate with insanity. And I'm asking myself, what's wrong with this picture?

Once I'm in my room with the door closed, the lump in my throat gets bigger. It makes me so sad to consider how things once were, how we can never go back. It's times like this when I miss Dad the most. And sometimes I wonder if he can see us now. And if he can see us, what does he think? Does it break his heart? Does it hurt him like it's hurting me?

But then I think that God must have a different way of showing things down here; He must do it in a more complete way. Like maybe Dad can see how things will be, like when things get better for us—surely they will get better. Because honestly, I don't see how heaven could be heaven if Dad was looking down and seeing how things really are—right now anyway. I think it would just kill him all over again.

I try to distract myself from these melancholy thoughts, as well as from my growing concern about Kayla, while I finish up the last of my homework. But finally I'm done and just turning out my light when Mom pokes her head into my room to check on me and to tell me she's home.

"Did you talk to Zach?" she asks.

"He was asleep."

"Oh…" She nods. "At least he's home."

"Yeah. Good night, Mom. I love you."

She smiles. "I love you too, Sam. Good night."

Then she closes the door, and I hear her going into her room. Worried that she might cry herself to sleep again tonight, I put in a good CD, turning it up just enough to drown out her sobs—just in case. Then I get into my bed and I pray. My theory about praying is that you can do it anywhere and everywhere, and if it makes you feel better to kneel by the side of your bed, then do it. If you prefer to stand on your head to pray, then do it. Most important, *just do it.*

After I've covered my family as best I can, I pray for Kayla again. I pray that God will keep her safe and get her home as quickly as possible. And then I go to sleep.

———

It's stifling hot in here. And dry. So dry that my nostrils are burning. And I am so thirsty that my mouth feels like it's stuffed with cotton.

Then I realize I can't even part my lips. It's as if they're glued together, but I can tell by the smell of vinyl that my mouth is taped shut.

It's too dark to see anything, other than a narrow strip of light over there. It must be a window draped with some- thing very dark. I lie on my side, on something lumpy and covered with fabric, maybe an old mattress. But it smells horrible. Like a dog, or worse.

My shoulder joints ache from my arms being stuck behind my back, but when I try to move, I realize that my wrists are bound together, so tightly that the skin feels raw and irritated. And my ankles are tied together as well.

I want to scream, to cry for help, but I am unable to do anything. All I can do is to lie here and wait. But for what? Why am I here? *Why am I here?*

I wake up with tears pouring down my cheeks and my heart pounding so hard it feels like I've been running for hours. I get out of my bed and turn on the light and look around. But I'm in my own room, and everything is just as it was before I went to bed.

Nothing is really wrong. It just feels wrong. All wrong.

It was only a dream. Rather, a nightmare. A horrible, horrible nightmare. The worst nightmare I've ever had. So real. So frightening.

I get back in bed and immediately begin to pray. "Dear God, please take away the horror of this nightmare. Replace it with Your perfect peace—the kind of peace that goes beyond my human understanding. Thank You. Amen."

I take several long, deep breaths. And finally, when I am calmed down, when my heart has returned to a normal pace and I can breathe without panting, I realize that the dream wasn't about me at all. It was about Kayla.

Kayla is in trouble. Very serious trouble.

I consider calling the police right now, but what would I tell them? That I've had a dream? How would that help anything? And so I earnestly pray for Kayla. I beg God to watch over her, to protect her, and to send help—*quickly*.

I get up early the next morning. And although it feels as if I've barely slept, I am wide awake. And I am asking God to show me what to do. I open my Bible to where it's marked from the last time I did my daily devotion. But instead of reading the next passage in John 18, my eyes are fixed on the verses at the top of the page, ones that I read yesterday—part of Jesus' prayer in the Garden before He was arrested.

But for some reason I feel that God wants me to take this personally. I read from John 17:15–18. It's as if Jesus is speaking specifically to me!

"I'm not asking that you take [her] out of the world

But that you guard [her] from the Evil One.

[She is] no more defined by the world Than I am defined by the world.

Make [her] holy—consecrated—with the truth;

Your word is consecrating truth.

In the same way that you gave me a mission in the world,

I give [her] a mission in the world."

I feel such a sense of power from these verses—as if God is telling me to go and to take care of what He's shown me in the dream I had last night, in the visions He gave me yesterday. Yet I'm not sure where to go or what to do. So I pray some more and ask for specific guidance. And just as I am finishing up, a name comes to mind.

Ebony.

Almost as clearly as if I had heard it spoken audibly, although I'm sure that I only heard it in my head. *Ebony*.

Now the only person I've ever known by the name of Ebony is the woman who was my dad's partner on the police force, just before he died. And while she seemed like a nice enough person, I never really got to know her well.

In fact, I've never told anyone this, but I've always been slightly suspicious of her. Like how did she manage to escape the bust-gone-bad without getting hurt? And wasn't she supposed to back up my dad? Naturally, these aren't the kinds of questions anyone expects a twelve-year-old to ask. Besides, there was so much else going on at the time...combined with the loss of Dad. I suppose I just sort of forgot about her. I think the last time I saw Ebony was at Dad's funeral, and she did stand up and say some very nice things about him. But then she should've since he was her partner.

Unfortunately, I can't even remember Ebony's last name right now. And I have no idea whether she still works for the police or not. But I get the distinct impression that I'm supposed to look this woman up. Hopefully God will show me just how I'm supposed to do this. Like do I call or e-mail or just walk into the precinct or what?

SIX

As Olivia drives us to school, I tell her about my
frightening dream, the new Bible verse, and finally my
impression to contact Ebony.

"Wow!" she says after I finish.

Once we're at school and getting out of her car, I have
to admit that in the light of day, just walking through the
parking lot toward school, where everyone is acting the
same as any other day, my story sounds pretty weird,
even to me. "I know… pretty freaky, huh?"

"So are you going to call Ebony?"

"I thought about it…but I don't even know her last
name or if she still works there. Talk about a cold call."

"Just call up the station and ask to speak to her." She
drops her keys in her purse then fishes out her cell phone
and hands it to me. "If she's not there, they'll tell you. And
if she is, well, how many Ebonys do you think there could
be anyway?"

I'm surprised that I still know the precinct number by
heart, and I carefully dial it, praying that I won't sound like
a basket case in the off chance that I actually get to speak
to Ebony.

"Ebony Hamilton?" a man asks after I've made my inquiry.

"Yes!" I say quickly, and it comes back to me: *Ebony Hamilton.*

"And this is regarding?"

"Uh, I'm a friend of Kayla Henderson, the girl who's missing."

"Hold on and I'll see if I can put you through to her."

"She still works there," I mouth to Olivia, who nods and smiles.

"This is Detective Hamilton," says a smooth, official-sounding female voice.

"Uh, this is Sam, I mean, Samantha McGregor. I'm not sure if you remember me or not, but—"

"Samantha McGregor," she says in a warmer tone. "Cliff's daughter. How are you?"

"Uh, I'm okay. I wasn't sure if you still worked there."

"I've been here for almost ten years now. I just made detective last year."

"Congratulations."

"Thank you. I'm sure your dad would've been higher than that by now. He was such a good cop."

"Yeah..." I take in a breath.

"So, what can I do for you, Samantha? The desk said that you were calling in regard to Kayla Henderson. Is she a friend of yours?"

"Well, yes. I mean, we used to be pretty good friends. But we've been more like casual friends these past couple of years."

"Uh-huh." I can hear a shuffling sound, like she's moving papers around, and I wonder if she thinks I'm just going to be wasting her time.

"Well, I might have some information…"

"Information on *Kayla*?"

"Yes. But it's kind of complicated to explain over the phone. And actually, it's almost time for class right now. Maybe I should make an appointment with you. If that's okay."

"Of course it's okay. What are you doing for lunch today?"

"Nothing. I mean, besides eating."

She laughs. "Can I pick you up at school?"

"In a police car?"

She laughs again. "Don't worry. I drive an unmarked car. It won't look like you're getting hauled off to jail."

I laugh too. "Actually, it used to be kind of thrilling when Dad would let me ride with him in the patrol car."

"But not so much now that you're older."

"Not so much."

So I tell her what time to pick me up and where, and then I hang up and hand the phone back to Olivia.

"That seemed to go okay," she says as she turns it off and puts it back in her bag.

"Yeah. Ebony actually sounded really nice."

"Any reason she shouldn't sound nice?"

"No," I say quickly. "Not really." We're just going into the building now, and this is a conversation that I'm not ready to start, or maybe even to have.

I don't begin to feel really nervous until fourth period. Fortunately, it's PE, and Mrs. Harper has us running our legs off on the basketball court. I think it's punishment for not going out for the girls' basketball team, which she coaches and which doesn't sound like it'll have much potential this year. But as a result of the many drills she puts us through, I don't have too much time to obsess over what I'm going to say to Ebony.

Of course, as we're getting dressed afterward, Olivia feels the need to remind me of my lunch date. "Do you have it sort of worked out?" she asks in a slightly hushed tone since Emma and Brittany are nearby. "I mean, do you have an idea about what you're going to tell her?"

I toss my sweaty PE clothes into my locker, slam it, then start shoving my feet into my boots. "Not really. I'm praying that God will lead me."

She nods. "I'll be praying too."

I'm dressed now, and it's time to head out to meet Ebony. I pull on my jacket and run my fingers through my slightly messy hair. "Here I go."

Olivia holds up crossed fingers. "See ya."

"Where's Samantha taking off to in such a big rush?" Emma asks as I head for the door.

"She's got a date," Olivia tells them in a mysterious voice.

"Who with?" asks Brittany.

"I'll bet she's meeting Conrad Stiles," says Emma. "I've heard he thinks she's hot."

I consider this comment as I hurry out of the locker room and through the breezeway that leads to the front of the school. Conrad's a nice enough guy, and from what I've heard a strong Christian too, but I had no idea he was into me—if he really is. Emma was probably just pulling my leg, I tell myself as I go past security and exit the main entrance.

Fortunately, we have open campus for lunch, so there's no need to check out. And I'm sure that if I'm late coming back, they would accept an excuse from a police detective. Not that I plan to be late.

I see a charcoal-colored Chevy sedan parked directly out front, and I'm sure it must be Ebony's, which seems ironic since it's not supposed to draw your attention. But because the vehicle is so plain and frumpy looking, it almost seems to scream *unmarked police car.* Really, they should be driving Honda Civics.

I squint, trying to see the driver through the passenger side window, but the tinting is so dark that I can't really tell. Then the driver side door opens, and an attractive African-American woman stands up and waves over the roof at me, and I know that it's Ebony. "Hey, Samantha."

"Hey," I call back as I go up to the car.

"Hop in."

I get into the car, which looks even more like a cop car on the inside, and buckle up.

"That tinted glass," she says as she pulls out, "makes it hard to see who's sitting inside. And considering your missing friend, I'm glad to see that you don't just hop into cars with strangers."

"Yeah, my dad made sure I had that one down when I was really little."

"Good for him." She's driving toward town now. "You mind if we eat at Rosie's?"

"That's fine." I remember the little deli my dad used to take me to occasionally. It's always been popular with cops. "I haven't been there in ages."

"It's so great to see you again, Samantha." She glances over at me and smiles. "You're looking really good. I don't think I've seen you since your dad's funeral."

"Yeah, I was thinking that same thing earlier today. That day seems like such a long time ago…sometimes anyway."

"That was a sad day…"

"Yeah. Losing him was pretty hard to take," I admit.

"For everyone."

"I never really heard much of the details of what happened that day—I mean, the day he got shot. I guess it was because I was only twelve, just a kid you know. Maybe no one thought I should hear about it."

"But you're curious now?"

"Yeah, wouldn't you be?"

She nods. "You bet I would."

"That's not why I called you today. But I guess… just because—"

"Would you like to hear my story about that day, Samantha?"

"I kinda would."

So she begins to tell me about how it was just a typical day. "It was midmorning, quiet, nothing much going on. We got the call at 10:43. A neighbor was complaining about the house next door and how they'd been making a lot of noise. We went in thinking it would just be a routine investigation— we'd write out a warning and be done with it. But when we got to the house, I got this feeling that something was amiss."

She glances at me now, almost as if she wants to see if I'm tracking with her. So I nod and she continues. "I told

Cliff that I was worried, but he didn't seem too concerned. And to be honest, it wasn't anything I could really put my finger on. Just a feeling, you know?"

"I know..."

"Anyway, we knocked on the front door, and no one answered. But we heard a grinding noise that seemed to be coming from beneath the house. So we walked around and discovered a side entrance with a steep, narrow stair-case that went down into what we figured must be a base-ment. The noise was coming from down there. I started to go down first, but Cliff said that he would lead the way. And since he was the senior officer, I didn't argue. But still I was worried. And although Cliff didn't remove his gun, I decided to have mine ready, just in case."

She takes a deep breath as she turns into the deli parking lot, then parks the car and shuts off the engine. She turns to me and removes her sunglasses. I can see tears in her eyes.

"It gets a little blurry here, Samantha. It all happened so fast. But Cliff knocked and no one answered. Then he tried the door and found it unlocked. He barely had it open when the shots went off. I shot and wounded the man with the gun. The other man just put his hands up, and then I called for backup. I did what I was trained to do, but I've never been so scared in my life. And the hardest thing I've ever seen was your dad just lying there, not moving."

She reaches over and puts her hand on my arm. "If I could've done anything differently...if I could've changed the outcome...I would've. I've played this scene over and

over in my head, and my only one regret is that I didn't listen to that feeling—that sense that something was wrong."

"Why didn't you?" I ask in a quiet voice.

"Because I'm a cop, Samantha. And I was a rookie cop
at that. We weren't trained to listen to our feelings. We
were trained to act and to react. To remain in control and
to follow the book. But now things are starting to change."
A faint smile lights up her dark brown eyes. "And in my line
of work, I've learned to rely on intuition even more."

She opens the car door. "You hungry?"

———

As we walk toward Rosie's, I mentally replay what she's
just told me. Although I'm relieved to hear some of this, it's
also really hard. I wasn't prepared for this. As we go inside
the deli, I'm surprised at how familiar it feels. I'm sure I
haven't been here since Dad was alive. It almost feels like
I'm going to start crying. I hope I don't. "Dad really liked
this place," I say in a slightly gruff voice as we step up to
the counter.

"Yeah, I know."

We place our order. I get the pastrami and Swiss on
rye, just like Dad used to. And then we go and sit down.

Ebony sighs and pushes a strand of auburn-tinted hair
away from her face. "Man, when I got up this morning I
sure hadn't planned on any of this. I can't believe I just told
you that whole story. I hope you don't mind that—"

"No," I say quickly. "I mean, it's not easy to hear, but I
do appreciate knowing what happened. I had wondered…"

"I would've if I were you."

I take a sip of my soda and try to decide where to begin.

"I'm surprised that you even knew I was handling Kayla's case. It was transferred to me from Detective Ramsay only late yesterday. He leaves on Friday for two weeks' vacation. How did you hear I had it?"

"I didn't."

She nods as she squeezes a wedge of lemon into her iced tea. "I remember your dad saying that you were gifted, Samantha. He told me that you and your grandmother had some things in common."

"Grandma McGregor?"

Ebony nods.

"She died a couple years ago."

"I'm sorry."

"She lived in Boston, and I didn't really know her very well. But I do remember Dad saying that I was like her. Of course, I thought that was pretty weird at the time. I mean, when you're just a kid and your dad tells you that you're like this old lady who's like seventysomething...well, you don't know how to respond."

Ebony chuckles. "Don't worry; he meant it as a compliment. His mother was a strong Christian woman with a gift for...you know, for seeing things. Your dad seemed to think that maybe you had it too."

I blink in surprise. "I didn't know that—I mean, about Grandma McGregor."

She nods. "That's what he told me. He had hoped you'd get to spend some time with her."

"I wish I'd gotten the chance." I shake my head. "I just never knew."

There's a quiet lull in our conversation now. So much to process, so much to take in. I study Ebony for a moment. It's weird, but in some ways she seems like a long-lost friend or a relative, and I'm so thankful that I'm getting to spend some time with her. But then just as our sandwiches are delivered, I remember the real reason I'm here.

"Mind if I ask a blessing?" she says.

"Not at all." I smile and bow my head as she says a quick but sincere-sounding prayer. Then I echo, "Amen."

"So what about Kayla?" She picks up her pickle spear, holding it like a torch. "What do you know, Samantha?"

"I was worried that what I have to say will sound really bizarre. But based on what you know about me, what you heard from my dad, well, maybe you'll understand."

"Go ahead," she says.

And so I do. But even as I tell her these strange things, and even as I go back to the notebook where I've been jotting them down—as if I might forget them, which seems absurd—I think it must sound pretty incredible. And my guess is that the other detective, the one who is going on vacation tomorrow, might've laughed or dismissed me as a lunatic. Finally I think I've pretty much said it all. "Pretty freaky, huh?"

She presses her lips together and slowly nods. "You've barely touched your sandwich, Samantha. Why don't you eat while I make some notes and write down questions about some of the things you just told me?"

So I take a break and begin eating my sandwich. I try not to stare as she jots stuff down. Finally I'm done, and I'm dying to hear her reaction. I mean, I doubt that she thinks I'm seriously crazy, but she might have some concerns.

"What do you think?" I ask her as I wipe my mouth with a napkin. "I should warn you that my mom sent me to a shrink last year. And I'd be worried about telling her any of this…for fear she'd send me back again."

Ebony nods. "I can understand that."

"Do you think I'm nuts?"

"No. I think you're gifted, Samantha."

"So, do you think this is real? Is it possible that God is trying to tell me something about Kayla? That she's really in trouble? Like my dream last night…do you think someone is holding her against her will?"

She frowns. "I think it's possible."

"But not likely?"

"I didn't say that. It's just that her mother seems pretty certain that Kayla ran off to be with her boyfriend."

"Colby in San Diego?"

She nods.

"The UCLA graduate with an apartment and a car and a good job?"

She nods again.

"Don't you think it's a little weird that someone like Colby would want to get involved with a sixteen-year-old? I mean, doesn't California have the same laws as Oregon about adults and minors?"

"Yes. But as you probably know, a lot of teens have fake IDs."

"So do you really think that Kayla is down in San Diego tying the knot with Prince Charming?"

"I already had my doubts..." She kind of smiles at me. "And after hearing your story, I have even more doubts."

"But I still haven't given you enough to do anything, right?"

She glances down at her notes. "Well, it's pretty sketchy, Samantha. I can't deny that. But these cases are like putting together a puzzle. It takes lots of pieces. And to be honest, these are some of the best pieces I've had so far."

"I heard that Kayla was seen getting onto a bus."

"Yes. We've contacted the bus company and requested their passenger list to LA and San Diego on Saturday, but so far no luck." Ebony looks at her watch. "Looks like you're going to be late, Samantha. Is that a problem?"

I grin at her. "Just for biology. No big deal."

She frowns then looks down at her notes. "But you had one of your visions about Kayla in biology, didn't you?"

"Oh yeah."

"Well, let's get you back." She places a tip on the table and stands. "I'm sure I still have your home phone number, but do you have a cell phone number where I can reach you?"

"I don't. But my best friend, Olivia, does."

"Why don't you write it down for me?" Then she pulls a business card out of her purse. "Here, this has my numbers

on it. Feel free to call if you come up with anything new."
She smiles at me. "Or if you just need to talk."

And as we go out to her "unmarked" car, I'm thinking
maybe I will call her—even if it is just to talk. Maybe she
gets me. Either that or she feels sorry for me and is worried that I'm going off the deep end. But I hope that's not
the case.

Seven

It's hard to concentrate during my afternoon classes. For one thing, I'm still replaying my conversation with Ebony…still amazed that she didn't question what I told her and that she seems to understand me. But even more than that, I'm thinking a lot about Kayla. I can't get last night's nightmare out of my head. It's like that horrifying image, those feelings of being bound and gagged, just won't go away.

But the part that's really bugging me is that I'm suddenly remembering the awful feeling of being so hot and dry and thirsty. Is it possible that there was a fire somewhere? That the building Kayla was trapped in was burning? And if so, is it possible that we'll be too late? On top of this, I realize that I didn't mention anything about the heat to Ebony today. There was so much else to tell that I guess it slipped my mind.

But by the time I'm in drama, I feel really worried. I'm tempted to borrow someone's cell phone to call Ebony, but Queen Gertrude has lines again today. As a result, I'm up onstage. We're in act 4, scene 7 now, and for some reason it's really getting to me. I'm sure the reason is that Ophelia (played by Kendall instead of Kayla) has died. And although it's only a play and something I wouldn't normally take too seriously, today it seems very real.

When the time comes for me to read my longest lines, the ones where Queen Gertrude describes the death of poor Ophelia, I am nearly in tears. I've read through these lines enough times to understand that I, the queen, am describing the scene of Ophelia's drowning, talking about the flowers that were floating on the water all around her, including "crow-flowers, nettles, daisies, and long purples…" And I describe the flower garlands that had fallen from her hair, and how her "clothes spread wide" and "mermaid-like" kept her afloat for a while as she sang her haunted songs. And finally I say, choking back a sob, "Till that her garments, heavy with their drink, pull'd the poor wretch from her melodious lay…*to muddy death.*"

Naturally, I'm totally embarrassed by this unexpected display of emotion, but to my surprise, Mr. Owens starts to clap, and then the others join him. And after the scene is finished, Mr. Owens approaches me and asks why I haven't participated in any of the past drama productions.

"I, uh, I don't know…"

"Well, I'd like to officially invite you to audition for our next play." He smiles hopefully.

"Thank you."

"It won't be until after the winter break, but there's a specific part I'd like to see you try for, Samantha. Will you consider it?"

"I guess."

"Good." He rubs his hands together. "You seem to have great intuitions."

I sort of nod. "Maybe so." Of course, I know he's referring to acting intuitions, but I can't escape the irony.

As I leave the auditorium, I feel more haunted than ever—haunted by Kayla. Reading that scene, so full of death and sadness and gloom, then remembering last night's dream, I suddenly feel very scared. What if Kayla is already dead? What if I didn't correctly receive God's messages, or if I hesitated too long? What if it's too late?

But then I remind myself as I walk toward the locker bay that I don't really see how I could've done anything differently. It was only last night that I received the dream, and I called the police this morning. Still, it's weighing on me. And the question that nags at me, tormenting me just like it did last winter, —what if I'm not up to this? What if I blow it?

"Hey, Sam," calls Olivia as she joins me. "How's *Hamlet*?"

"Don't ask." I toss a dark scowl at her.

"Depressing stuff, huh?"

I glance over my shoulder to make sure no one's listening. "Ophelia died today."

"Did you see Kayla again?" she asks in a quiet voice.

"No. But when I had to read my part, which goes into detail about Ophelia's drowning, well, I kind of lost it."

She pats me on the back. "Sorry..."

"Yeah. The upside is that Mr. Owens thinks I'm a real actress now."

She kind of laughs. "Maybe you are."

"Yeah, right. The only reason I fell apart was because I kept thinking about Kayla." Then I tell her about how I forgot to mention part of my dream to Ebony today. "I didn't tell her about the heat, and now I'm thinking, what if the place was on fire? Or what if it's going to be on fire? What if Kayla is in real danger?"

Olivia digs in her purse and hands me her phone. "Go ahead and tell her."

I wait until we're outside to call Ebony. But I get her voice mail and am forced to leave a message, which I'm sure must sound pretty crazy. But at least it's off my mind, for now.

Then as Olivia is driving toward my house, her phone rings. She answers it then hands it to me. "It's Ebony Hamilton."

"Sorry to call on your friend's phone," Ebony begins. "But I figured you wouldn't be home yet."

"Did you get my message?"

"No. Did you have another vision?"

So I retell her the message. "It might not be anything, but it just got me really worried."

"I appreciate it. The reason I called was to see if you were busy this afternoon."

"Not really. Olivia was just taking me home and—"

"Would she mind dropping you off at Kayla's house instead?"

"I, uh, I guess not. Why?"

"I spoke to Kayla's mom and asked if it would be okay for you to spend some time in Kayla's room."

"In Kayla's room?"

"I know it sounds weird, but I was reading a little about psychics this afternoon, and I—"

"I'm not a psychic, Ebony." I know my voice sounds harsh, but I just want to make sure this is totally clear.

"I know that, Samantha. I'm sorry. I shouldn't have used that word. But you do have a certain gift. I'm just not sure what it's called."

"I'm not either. But I just don't like the idea of being called a psychic. That stirs up these horrible images of wild-eyed women wearing too many scarves and shawls and big hoop earrings, peering into their crystal balls and reading their astrology charts and...well, *you know*?"

She sort of laughs. "I totally understand."

"And that's not what this is." I glance over at Olivia, who looks like she's suppressing laughter too. "Just for the record, I do not believe in Ouija boards or horo-scopes or tarot cards or any of that crud."

"*I know*, Samantha. But just hear me out, okay? I did a little research, and I read that sometimes it helps a *gifted* type of person to make a connection with someone if you're around that person's things or where they spent time. And you said yourself that two of your visions happened in classes Kayla had shared with you. During biology class and then in drama. Remember?"

"Yes."

"So, I called Mrs. Henderson, and without telling her too much, I asked if we could come and spend some time in Kayla's room. Are you game?"

"Okay, as long as you don't tell Kayla's mom that I'm a psychic."

"Don't worry. I told her I was bringing a helper. I was thinking that, if you don't mind, maybe I could tell her you're an intern. We could call you that, Samantha. We could even make it semiofficial. If it would make this easier for you."

"Sure, that'd be fine. I just don't think I could stand it if everyone started to think I had psychic powers, you know?"

"Right. Anyway, I'm in my car now, and I could be at Kayla's in about ten minutes. Can you meet me there?"

I glance at Olivia. "Do you mind dropping me at Kayla's?"

"No problem."

"Sure," I tell Ebony. "We're about fifteen minutes from the Hendersons' now."

So Olivia does a U-turn at the next intersection, and we go back across town. "Sorry about that."

"It's okay, Samantha. This if for Kayla, remember? It's important."

Ebony's car is already parked in front, and I tell Olivia just to drop me off. "Thanks for the ride."

"Let me know how it goes."

I nod and then slowly walk to the front door, taking my time as I study the older ranch style house, wondering how Kayla might've felt when she walked down this path. I knock at the door and brace myself for Mrs. Henderson. I'm sure she'll have questions, wondering why I've suddenly decided to become an intern for Ebony. I figure I can use my dad as an excuse, say that I've always been interested in police work, which isn't entirely untrue.

But it's Ebony who opens the door. "Mrs. Henderson had an appointment. She said to make ourselves at home."

"Good."

"Now, I'm not sure what's best to do," she begins. "But I definitely don't want to get in your way. I'm thinking that maybe you should just walk around without me to distract you. Just see if you sense anything."

I nod. "That sounds like a good plan."

"And I'll just stay in the living room." She sits on the couch. "But I'll be praying for you."

"Cool. That'll probably be more helpful than anything."

I take off my backpack, and after removing my notebook and pen, I set the pack by the door. "Just in case I need to write anything down," I tell her.

"Good thinking."

I've only been to Kayla's house a few times, and that was back in middle school. But I still remember the general layout and where her bedroom is. Even so, I feel very strange and out of place as I walk through the quiet and dimly lit house. I have no idea what I should be doing, what I should be looking for, or if I should even be looking at all. I mean, I know better than anyone that this isn't about seeing with physical eyes.

So I just stand in the middle of the hallway that goes to her bedroom, and I begin to pray. I ask God to show me anything that will help us to help Kayla. One thing I feel certain of—Kayla is in need of our help.

Then I continue on into her room. The door is open, but I feel like a trespasser as I go inside. I know how I would hate to have anyone snooping around my room. Not that I plan to snoop. I don't. I'm just not sure what I plan to do.

The full-sized bed has been stripped, and the naked mattress gives this space an abandoned feeling. I'm not sure why it's been stripped, but I'm guessing it has to do with the investigation. Maybe it's because they originally suspected a kidnapping.

Her closet door is open, and although a lot of clothes are still hanging there, I see the empty spaces, where I'm sure she removed the things she wanted to take with her to San Diego.

Her dresser has the regular things on it. A few photos. One that was actually taken during middle school. I'm surprised to see it and bend down to study it. It was taken at the youth camp where I rededicated my life to God. Kayla, Olivia, and I are standing with some other girls, smiling as if we'd never been happier. I shake my head to get rid of those distracting memories. That's not why I'm here.

Then I see a photo of Kayla and Parker, dressed formally, I'm guessing it was for prom. It was obviously taken before Emma stepped into the picture and messed things up for all of them, although as I recall it wasn't long afterward. Kayla looks so pretty. Some blondes don't look good in red, but she can carry it off with those striking brown eyes. And I'm sure she could pass for twenty-one too. Especially if she had a fake ID. Still, this is not why I'm here.

Finally I sit on her bed, lay my notebook in my lap, and just close my eyes. I take in a deep breath, and I start praying for Kayla. The words come easily. Mostly I pray for her safety, that we will locate her soon, and that as a result of whatever is going on, she will call out to God for help.

Then I take another deep breath and just wait.
I quiet my heart and wait to see if God is going to show
me anything. But nothing happens. And after about ten
minutes, I feel like I'm just wasting my time. And Ebony's.

I go out to the hallway and call to her. "I don't think this
is working."

She comes over to join me. "Well, it was worth a try."

"Do you think it's okay if I use the bathroom before we go?"

"Of course. Mrs. Henderson said to make ourselves
at home."

So I go into the bathroom across from Kayla's room and
use the toilet. Then as I turn off the faucet after washing my
hands, I look up at the mirror above the sink and I experience that familiar flash of light. I hardly dare to breathe as I
stare into the mirror and wait. But instead of seeing my own
image, I see Kayla's face—at least I think it's her face. It's
kind of blurry and dark, as if the sun is coming from directly
behind her. Then I look beyond her and see what appears to
be the silhouette of mountains. Very rugged looking mountains that are copper colored. I blink and try to see it better,
but in the same instant it's gone. So quickly that I wonder if it
was real. But I know it was. Still, what does it mean?

"Mountains," I mutter to myself as I walk through the
house, finally stopping by the front door, where Ebony is
waiting with my backpack.

"Did you say something?" she asks.

I quickly open my notebook and look back through my
recent notes until I find the place where I wrote out the Scripture that I found in Jeremiah the other day. I find the part I'm

looking for and read it aloud. "'They abandoned them in the mountains where they wandered aimless through the hills.'"

"And? What does that mean?"

"I just saw Kayla in the bathroom," I begin with excitement. "I mean, she wasn't *in* the bathroom, but I was looking in the mirror and I saw her image there. But it was kind of blurry and dim, and the sun was shining behind her, and there were mountains behind her too. Copper-colored mountains that looked really rocky and rugged and jaggedy. Not like the ones we have here in Oregon, at least not the ones I've seen." I open to a clean page of my notebook and attempt to sketch what they looked like, then hold it up for her to see.

"Hmm…" Ebony studies my pathetic-looking drawing and nods.

"Well, I'm not much of an artist, but if I saw a photo of something that looked similar, I think I could identify it."

"Doesn't look much like San Diego."

"Maybe someplace near there?"

"Maybe…" She looks at me. "Anything else?"

"That was it. Not much, huh?"

"It might be another piece of the puzzle, Samantha."

"I just wish there weren't so many pieces. Why can't God just show me the whole thing at once?"

She kind of laughs as she opens the door. "What would be the fun in that?"

"But what if Kayla's in danger?"

"I guess we'll just have to trust God for that too." She locks the door, then slips the key underneath a flowerpot off to the right. "You can only see as much as God wants to show you. And there might even be a reason for this delay. I've come to learn that God's timing is a lot better than ours."

"I just hope she's okay."

"So do I."

Ebony asks about my family as she drives me home.

"We've definitely had our ups and downs," I admit.

"I'm sure it hasn't been easy."

"Mom works a lot, and Zach's been in rehab a couple of times. Once for alcohol, once for drugs."

"I'm sorry."

"Me too."

"You guys have been in my prayers," she says as she turns down my street. "To be honest, a lot more right after your dad was killed. But you'll be in them a lot more now."

"Thanks."

"And go easy on yourself, Samantha."

"What do you mean?"

"Like I said at Kayla's house. You can only know what God wants you to know. If He's not showing you every-thing, then you'll just have to trust Him for it."

"I know...but I guess I kind of feel responsible too. Like He's placed this huge burden on me, and maybe I'm the only one who knows what's going on with Kayla. And yet I don't know much of anything. Or maybe I'm not listening well enough."

"I think you're doing just fine, Samantha. And I'm going to share my favorite Scripture with you. I'm sure you've heard it before, but I think you may need to hear it again. Okay?"

"Okay."

She pulls up at my house and turns and looks at me. "It's Philippians 4:6–7, and I glommed on to it shortly after your dad died. I used to say it to myself over and over throughout the day. Now it's more of just a once-a-day thing. I memorized it in King James Version. Here goes. 'Be careful for nothing; but in every thing by prayer and supplication with thanksgiving let your requests be made known unto God. And the peace of God, which passeth all understanding, shall keep your hearts and minds through Christ Jesus.'"

I nod. "Yeah, I'm familiar with that verse."

"Good. You might want to memorize it too. And then I'm going to challenge you to really think about what it says. It doesn't just say to simply pray, Samantha. It says to make *supplications*, which means to really beat on God's door. And then it also says to thank God. And I've come to believe that means we need to thank Him even before we see the answers to our prayers. You know what I mean?"

I smile at her. "I'm surprised you're a cop, Ebony. Did you ever consider being a pastor?"

She laughs. "Actually, my daddy was a preacher man."

"Was?"

"He died when I was fifteen."

"Oh…"

Just then her cell phone rings, and I'm not sure whether to get out of the car or to wait to say good-bye. But she motions me to stay put.

"Is that so?" she says into the phone. "Very interesting."

She glances at me and nods. "Well, thank you very much, Eric." Then she hangs up. "Guess what?"

"What?"

"Kayla never went to San Diego at all."

"Really?"

"The bus company did a little more research, and it turns out she bought a ticket to Phoenix."

"Phoenix?"

She nods. "And those mountains you drew…"

"Phoenix?"

"That's what I'm thinking. I've only been down to Arizona once, but they have some spectacular mountains there. Some that are all jagged and cut up like the ones you drew today."

"And the heat and dryness?" I ask hopefully. "Maybe it's not a fire?"

"It can get pretty hot down there. Especially if you're in a place without air-conditioning."

"So where do you begin to search for her in Phoenix?" I ask.

"Well, we send all the information we have down there, and then we pray for a miracle."

"And that God will give me some more clues?"

"That's what I'm going to be praying."

And so as I walk into the house, I feel slightly encouraged. It seems that I'm really on the trail after all. And, I remind myself, it's God who's doing the leading here. It won't do any good for me to get impatient.

Eight

By Friday, it's been nearly a week since Kayla left town. Not to San Diego like we all thought, but to Phoenix. I'm amazed at how quickly this new bit of information sweeps through our school. Apparently it was on the news last night, an attempt to jog some memories and warm up what seems to be turning into a cold case. And it must be working because today Kayla seems to be the hot topic of the locker room again.

"So, if Kayla's in Phoenix," Brittany says as she pulls on her jeans, "then whatever happened with that Colby dude she was supposed to marry down in San Diego?"

I'm not sure who she's directing this question to, but I decide to field it myself. "Does anyone really know for sure that there ever was a Colby dude?" And now the locker room grows quieter. "I mean, did anyone ever see a photo of him? Did you see any of the e-mails she got from him?"

"Well, you remember what Kayla told us last fall," says Emma. "How she met him in San Diego. Are you saying she made that up?"

"Well, the search for him in San Diego has come up empty," Olivia points out. "And the newspaper said that Kayla's aunt had never heard of him."

"Besides," I remind them, "Kayla didn't go to San Diego. Remember?"

"But she went of her own free will to Phoenix," says Brittany. "Maybe she was going to meet Colby in Phoenix."

"Maybe Colby moved," adds Emma.

We continue speculating, going round and round, but mostly we don't land anywhere. And then it's lunchtime, and since it's Friday, Olivia and I are heading over to Sushi-Yaki to celebrate the end of the week.

Olivia's older sister, Clair, and her husband opened up this little restaurant about a year ago, and they're struggling to make a go of it. We do our best to support them by eating there on Fridays. It's not that I'm into sushi, but I do like their teriyaki.

"You know what I'm starting to think?" I ask Olivia after we visit with Clair and place our orders and sit down.

"About what?"

"About Kayla."

"What?"

"I'm thinking that she made up that whole bit about Colby."

"Why?"

"Well, I was thinking about when Kayla told us about meeting this guy, back in October when we were setting up the photo exhibit for the fall art fair. Emma had been going on and on about Parker this and Parker that. They were still dating then, and I could tell that it was bugging Kayla. Then suddenly she just started talking about this really cool guy she met in San Diego. And, well, it just sounded a little too convenient. Not only that, but he sounded a little too good to be true."

"And you know what they say about that."

"If it's too good to be true, it's not usually true."

"But what about the e-mails with the name Colby?" she asks.

"That's just the thing. I was really trying to remember the conversation back in October, and to be honest, I can't say that I remember everything. But I do not recall her saying a name. In fact, I think that's what made me a little suspicious even then. I mean, how do you go on and on about a guy but never mention his name?"

"Does seem a little weird."

"Here you go, ladies." Dan, Clair's husband, sets our orders on the table. "Anything else?"

"Looks good," says Olivia.

"Enjoy." He wipes his hands on the front of his apron and grins.

Then we bow our heads and silently pray. But just as I'm thinking *Amen*, I experience another flash of light—and suddenly I see a guy wiping his hands on the front of apron just like Dan did. But it's not Dan. This guy is a lot heavier than Dan. And older too. But I also see a name tag on the apron, one that's embroidered right into it. And it says *Colby*.

"Olivia!" I say with wide eyes. "I just saw him!"

"Jesus?" Olivia asks with a puzzled look.

"No. Colby!"

"Huh?"

So I explain what just happened, in detail, and Olivia digs in her purse then hands me her phone.

"Maybe I should get a cell phone of my own," I mutter as I dial Ebony's number.

"Hello?"

"Sorry if I'm interrupting your lunch," I tell her. "Although something just interrupted mine. Something I thought you should hear about."

"Tell me."

So I try to explain the vision I just had.

"Did you see the face of this guy, Samantha?"

"Kind of. But I don't know how to describe it exactly. Except that he was old."

"How old?"

"Like thirtysomething."

She sort of laughs. "That old, eh?"

"Well, you know…"

"So what was it about him that made you think he was old?"

"Well, I'm not sure." I try hard to remember. "But it seems as if he was sort of balding. I mean, he had hair, but maybe it was a receding hairline. And he just seemed older."

"Can you draw a picture of him?"

I laugh. "Yeah, right. You saw my mountain-scape."

"I know—I'd like to put you together with Michael."

"Michael?"

"Michael Taylor. A criminal composite artist I recently heard about. He's supposed to be amazingly good. I'll call and see if he's available. I think he lives in Portland. Can I call you back on Olivia's phone?"

I glance at Olivia but know she'll agree. "Yeah, I'm sure Olivia won't mind. Although she might start charging me for minutes."

"Maybe we should get you a cell phone of your own," Ebony says suddenly. "Just for official use, of course."

"Oh, I don't know."

"Well, I'll get back to you. Keep Olivia's phone on."

I hang up and tell Olivia about Ebony's plan.

"This is so exciting, Samantha. It's like God is really using you to find Kayla. Doesn't it feel cool?"

I consider this. "Sometimes it does. But sometimes not so much. I mean, sometimes I get worried or scared or freaked that I'm going to mess up. And then I try to remember that God's in control and that He's calling the shots. But it's not all fun and games, you know."

"Yeah, but it's still cool."

"I guess."

We finish our lunch, and Ebony hasn't called back. "Do you want to keep my phone?"

"No," I tell her. "It's your phone."

"Like I'm getting any important calls." She laughs. "Not like I have any kind of hot social life going on."

"You and me both."

"Oh, that reminds me," she says as we get in her car. "I have Conrad Stiles in English, and he was asking me about you."

"About me?"

"Yeah. And I thought it was interesting since Emma recently mentioned that she thought he was into you."

"That's just weird."

"Conrad is a cool guy, Samantha. Are you saying you wouldn't be interested in getting to know him better?"

"No..." I think about this. "He is a cool guy. And I'm pretty sure he's a strong Christian too. I guess it's just hard to take seriously. Like what was he asking you about?"

She snickers. "He wanted to find out if you were like Hannah Thornton."

"Hannah Thornton? What do you mean by that? I mean, I know she's a strong Christian, but we're not really anything alike."

"Hannah doesn't date, remember?"

"Oh yeah."

"He wanted to know your dateability status. He thought maybe you were like Hannah in that regard?"

"As in, have I kissed dating good-bye too?"

She laughs.

"Well, I suppose it's okay if some people want to think that. It makes a good reason for not dating."

"Not if it's not true."

"Maybe not. But it's not like I went out and told anyone that either."

"So, anyway, what do you want me to tell him, Sam?"

I laugh nervously. "Tell him that I'm very picky."

"That's good."

"And that I'd have to get to know a guy as a friend first."

"Uh-huh. That's good too."

"And," I'm trying not to laugh now, "you can tell him that I've taken an abstinence pledge, and I won't be having sex until marriage."

"Yeah, you bet, Samantha. Like I'm going to tell him *that*!"

"Just testing."

"Thanks a lot."

"Oh, I don't care what you tell him, Olivia. It's not like it's going to matter anyway."

"So, you don't want to go out with him?"

I shrug. "I don't know…maybe I *should* be like Hannah. It might be easier not to get involved with a guy. I mean, look at Kayla."

"Good point."

"Tell him whatever you want," I say now. "As long as it's true, that is."

"Okay."

"Just make sure you report back to me afterward."

"Aha. See, I knew you were interested."

"Hey, I'm only human."

Then Olivia starts talking about Alex Fontaine, a guy who just happens to be Conrad's best friend. And suddenly I am putting two and two together.

"You like Alex, don't you?"

"Oh, I don't know…"

"You do, Olivia!" I turn and stare at my best friend. "I know you do!"

"What? Did you just have a vision or something?"

"No, but I can see things with my eyes too. And your cheeks are getting red."

Her hand flies up to her face. "Are not."

"Are too!"

And for the rest of the short ride to school, we argue over whether or not Olivia has a crush on Alex. And by the time we get there, I'm pretty sure she does. Now I'm teasing her mercilessly. It's fun to see Olivia squirm.

"Can you just stop?" she asks as we get out of her car.

I'm laughing now. "Stop what?"

"You know what."

"Okay." We're barely inside the school when I spot Alex and Conrad. "There he is," I whisper to Olivia. "Lover boy."

She turns around and glares at me. *"Enough."*

"Okay." I nod. And I can tell she's had enough. "Sorry," I say quickly.

"You better be." Then we walk past Conrad and Alex, but as they say hi, I get the feeling that they were watching us the whole time. And I'm thinking, *Hey, this could be fun.*

Still, as I hurry to biology, I remind myself of what happened to Kayla. I think of how complicated her life got when she started dating and dating and dating. And I think of how she fell away from God the more she got involved. And then how she started going with Parker, her true love, and how she and Emma got into that horrible fight over a boy. And finally, as I'm sitting in my seat, staring at Kayla's empty chair in front of me, I think about how she disappeared only a week ago. And how I feel certain that she's in some kind of serious trouble. If that's what having a boyfriend gets you, well, count me out. Maybe I will follow Hannah Thornton's example and kiss dating good-bye myself!

Nine

It's not until school ends that Olivia informs me that Ebony called for me during sixth period. "I thought I'd find you before seventh, but I was running late. Anyway, she left a message for you to stop by the precinct after school. Want me to drop you off?"

"Do you mind?"

"No. Actually, I'm sort of curious about why she wants to see you."

"Maybe she got ahold of the artist guy, and we're going to create beautiful pictures together."

"Well, promise to call me if anything new develops," Olivia tells me as she drops me in front of the police station. "Or call if you need a ride."

"Thanks." As I walk up the steps to the station, I realize that I haven't been here in years. I pause on the top step and just stand there. I have this very strong feeling that my dad is nearby. And okay, it might just be because the only times I was ever here had to do with him. Or maybe he really is.

"Going in, miss?" a uniformed officer holds the front door open for me.

"Thanks," I tell him as I go inside. Still, I want to hold on to that feeling, that sense that Dad was here, that maybe he's helping to watch over me. I wish he could give me some clues about Kayla. But maybe God doesn't work like that.

"I'm here to see Detective Hamilton," I tell the middle-aged woman at the front desk.

"Your name?"

"Samantha McGregor."

She looks up at me. "Cliff's little girl?"

I study her for a moment then nod.

"You don't remember me, do you, honey?"

I shake my head.

"I'm Bernice Waters. I knew your dad for years."

"Oh yeah. I do remember you. But I never saw you at this desk before."

"Just sitting in for one of the girls. We gotta help each other out, you know." Then she tells me how to find Ebony, and I wander back past the familiar desks and cubicles. Not much has changed since the last time I was here. I pause by the desk that my dad used to sit at. Relieved that no one is here right now, I run my hand over the top of it and just remember.

"Samantha," Ebony says as she comes around the corner. "I was hoping I wouldn't miss you. I just got here." She pauses as she realizes where I'm standing then slowly nods. "Yeah, that's right where your dad sat," she says in a lowered voice. "Officer Parks uses that desk now. He's a good guy too." Then she pats me on the back. "Let's head on down to my office. Want a soda or anything?"

We stop by the soda machine, and I'm surprised that it too looks just the same. I feel like I've stepped into a time warp. Ebony gets me a Pepsi and a Diet Pepsi for herself; then we go into her office and sit down.

"I spoke to Michael Taylor right after you called at lunchtime."

"Is he here?"

"No. He can't come until tomorrow morning. Will that work for you?"

I nod.

"Hang on, let me tell Eric to put that call through to Michael and get it all set up."

So I sit here and sip my soda as she takes care of the details. But the whole time I'm thinking about Dad. I'm thinking that he's glad I'm here. That he's watching over me.

"There," she says. "That's settled. Now I want to tell you what Michael told me." She pulls out a notepad. "He faxed me some questions to ask you while the image is still fairly fresh in your head. Do you mind?"

"Not at all."

"Okay now, let me warn you…Michael is, well, he's a little unconventional. Not exactly what you'd call a psychic, and I know you don't like that word. But he relies more on feelings than facts. Do you understand what I mean?"

"I'm not sure."

"Well, he wanted you to just close your eyes while I ask you some questions. Are you okay with that?"

"Sure. Whatever." I lean back into the chair and close my eyes. "But I'll warn you," I say in a teasing tone. "I'm

feeling kinda sleepy right now; I hope I don't nod off
on you."

"This isn't supposed to be hypnosis. Michael said
you're supposed to just breathe and quiet yourself for a
minute or so. He said for me to tell you to just empty your
head of all distractions and just try to relax."

"You sure this isn't hypnosis?" I ask with one eye open.

"I know…it probably sounds weird, Samantha. But I'm
just following his instructions. To be honest, I've worked
with composite artists before, but Michael's technique is
new to me too. I'm interested to see if it works."

Then she proceeds to ask me a lot of questions that
seem pretty unrelated to anything. But I try to relax, and I
try to answer as best I can.

"Okay," she tells me. "That's all."

"Do you think that will really help?"

"I hope so."

"Me too."

"Another thing." She reaches into her desk. "This is for
you." She hands me a cell phone. "It's so we can stay in
touch without using all of your friend's minutes."

"Thanks." I flip open the phone. "This is nice."

"It has unlimited minutes. The phone number is written
on a sticker on the side. I've already put it into my instant
dial. And while it's for official use, no one will mind if you use
some of those free minutes for yourself. Just make sure you
don't tie it up too much."

"Don't worry; I'm not much of a phone person, and I
really don't have that much of a social life anyway."

She laughs. "Yeah, tell me another one, Samantha. A pretty girl like you?"

"Seriously, I mostly just hang with Olivia, and we go to youth group and school stuff. I'm not really a social butterfly or anything."

"No boyfriend?"

I shake my head. "Although I was thinking about it today."

"*Thinking* about it?"

"Yeah. There's this guy who might be interested in me."

"A nice guy?"

I nod. "I think so."

She smiles. "So, what's the problem then?"

"I'm just not sure I'm ready for that. I mean, yeah, I'm almost seventeen, and I've gone out like twice, and both times were pretty pathetic. But this whole thing with Kayla is kind of unnerving. I sure don't want to end up like her."

"She was kind of boy crazy, huh?"

"Yeah. But not always. Like before her parents split up, she was just a normal girl. She was a Christian and even went to youth group regularly. But she changed."

"Too bad."

"In fact, that reminds me of something. I already told Olivia about it today, and I made some notes in my notebook. It's not like a vision or anything, just something I remembered. Maybe another piece of the puzzle."

"Hit me."

So I tell her my memory of the day when Kayla started bragging about the San Diego boyfriend. "But I don't remember her ever mentioning his name that day. And I recall thinking it was kind of weird. At the time it made me suspect that maybe she was just putting on an act, to sort of show up Emma or maybe just to get her to shut up about Parker."

Ebony is making note of this. "Have you asked Emma about it?"

"No. It just hit me today."

"Do you mind if I ask Emma how she remembers it?"

"Not at all."

"As you know, we came up with zip-zero-nothing down in San Diego. Kayla's aunt couldn't confirm anything. And now that we know about this Arizona connection, well, we might've been chasing a wild goose in California all along."

"So, I was thinking..." I say. "If Kayla made up that whole story about the San Diego boyfriend, Mr. Perfect, but there was a guy in her e-mail named Colby, maybe she just wanted us to think it was the same guy. I mean, the made-up guy suddenly becomes her e-mail boyfriend. And then we all just assumed he lived in San Diego."

Ebony nods. "I was sort of thinking along those lines too, Samantha, especially after your vision of the guy in the apron with the name Colby on the front. Still, it's going to be like finding a needle in a haystack with the few facts we have so far. Phoenix is a huge place. I think it's closing in on 1.5 million now. But what makes it even worse is that it's one of the fastest growing cities in the country. In other words, it's a great place to hide."

"Oh..."

Ebony smiles as she stands, and I get the impression that she has someplace else to be about now. "But don't let that discourage you. We're making really good progress. And I can't wait to see what you and Michael come up with tomorrow. Do you need a ride home or anything?"

"Olivia told me to call her."

"Does she know about all this?"

I nod. "Yeah, I kinda need someone to talk to."

"Do you talk to your mom much? I mean, about things like this?"

"Not about this." I pull my jacket back on and pick up my pack. "It'd just freak her."

"So she doesn't know about your involvement in this case yet?"

I shake my head.

"She needs to know, Samantha. In fact, because you're a juvenile, she'll have to sign off in order for you to give evidence tomorrow."

"Oh…"

"Do you mind if I call her and have a little chat?"

"I guess not."

"I'll try not to freak her out."

"Thanks."

"Is it okay to call her at work?"

"Sure."

"She's still with the park district?"

"Yeah. Like about sixty hours a week."

We're walking down the hall now. "We'll need you here around nine tomorrow. Do you need a ride?"

"I'll ask Olivia if she can bring me."

"Olivia sounds like a good friend."

I nod. "She is."

Then I tell Ebony good-bye and use my new cell phone to call Olivia. I wait for her outside, but I'm surprised at how cold it's suddenly getting. I dig my wool scarf out of my backpack and wrap it around my neck. It almost feels like snow is in the air. I wonder what the temperature is in Phoenix. I'm guessing hot. Really hot.

Then I think about the fact that Ebony is going to call my mom, maybe even right now. I can't imagine how my mom will react to this. But I have a feeling that, although she'll probably be cool as can be with Ebony, she will be freaking underneath it all. And so while I wait, I pray.

Dear God, please help to smooth this out with my mom. I know she's got a lot of stress right now, and I don't want to add to her pile. Please, help her to understand this—and not to freak.

Ten

Okay, maybe I'm just a big chicken, but when Olivia invites me to spend the night at her house, I jump at the chance. Not that it's so unusual. I spend the night at her house at least a couple of times a month. And the fact that Mom might be in a huff after Ebony calls her, well, that's probably somewhat motivating too. Who can blame me?

"Let me pick up some things at my house," I tell Olivia. "And leave Mom a note. She probably won't get off work until late anyway. She said they're working to put something together for the Christmas parade tomorrow."

"I'm surprised she didn't rope you into it this year."

"After last year?"

Olivia laughs. "You made a cute Mrs. Santa."

"Yeah, right. Half the kids thought I was just an overgrown female elf."

"So she let you off easy this year?"

"Yeah, we cut a deal," I admit as she pulls into my driveway. "I get to do all her Christmas cards this year."

I'm relieved that nobody's home. And hopefully this means Zach actually went to work today. Friday is a busy day at the video store, and I'm guessing if Zach does another no-show, he'll probably lose his job. Then Mom will be furious.

I gather up some of my things and write Mom a quick note, just like I usually do on nights like this. No big deal. Yet for some reason, I feel kind of guilty. Like I'm trying to escape something, which I suppose is partially true.

Then I remind myself that I'm not really doing anything wrong. Mom has always been perfectly fine with me staying at Olivia's. In fact, I think she enjoys having our house to herself sometimes. It's just that I'm sure she'll want to talk to me after Ebony tells her about how I'm helping on the case. So I take the time to explain in my note about my new cell phone and why Ebony gave it to me. And I even write down the number so Mom can call me if she wants. Although I'm hoping she won't. What more can I do?

"Want to pick up a DVD?" Olivia asks as I get in the car. "I heard that movie just came out, the one you wanted to see with Reese Witherspoon."

"Okay."

So Olivia swings by the video store, the one my brother is supposed to be working at. But I don't see his old beater in the parking lot. Hopefully he's parked it in back. When we go inside, I don't see Zach. And when we get to the counter, I ask if he's there.

"No." The girl rolls her eyes as she gives us our change and receipt. "And he's in trouble now."

"Sorry," I tell her. But mostly I'm sorry for Zach.

"Do you think he'll get fired?" Olivia asks as we head for her car.

"Probably."

"Let's pray for him," Olivia says once we're in the car.

We bow our heads and really pray for Zach. We ask God to get his attention, to wake him up, to protect him, and to bring the right kinds of friends into his life—all kinds of things. Then finally we say amen.

"Sometimes it's hard to have faith when it comes to my own family," I admit as Olivia starts to drive.

"Yeah, I know. It's like that with Clair and Dan."

"Well, at least Clair and Dan aren't a mess."

"Not so you'd notice. But I hear Clair saying things about their marriage to my mom sometimes. Things that worry me."

"I just don't see why people want to make it so hard on themselves," I say. "I mean, it's so much easier to live with God than without Him."

"Yeah, you should know. You've had firsthand experience," teases Olivia. "And back then I used to wonder the same thing about you. Like why did you want to go to so much trouble just to be miserable? You know?"

"I guess it's just one of those things that some of us have to walk through before we get it. Maybe that's what's happening with Zach...and Clair and Dan too."

"I shouldn't talk. I suppose it could happen to me too."

"Nah," I tell her. "I think you're one of the smart ones, the kind who will hold on to God no matter what and never let go."

"I hope so. For both of us."

"Me too."

Olivia lives in a pretty nice neighborhood. Not that my neighborhood is exactly a slum. It's not. Just more middle class. Whereas Olivia's is more upper-crust. Her dad is a city attorney, and her mom is a part-time social worker for the county.

Olivia's the youngest of three kids. Even so, she's not spoiled. Not at all. I'm not even sure why. I could assume it's because her parents raised her right, but I'm thinking it has more to do with who she is. In fact, if any of the three kids were spoiled, I'd say it's her brother Edward, and he's the middle kid, so go figure.

But it's always a pleasure to be at Olivia's house. And that's not just because they have money. It has more to do with Olivia's mom. Mrs. Marsh is one of those women who loves doing "home things." Seriously, I think she and Martha Stewart could be related. Only Mrs. Marsh, in my opinion, is lots nicer.

So when you come to Olivia's house, you can always count on certain things. Like the house always looks gorgeous, there are usually good things to eat, and most of the time music is playing. Mrs. Marsh is the kind of person who will light candles *just because*.

And tonight when Olivia pulls up to their house, I'm not surprised that their Christmas lights, all white, are neatly hung and there's a big evergreen wreath on the glossy red front door. Not overly done. Just classy and right. And when Olivia parks her car in their big quadruple-wide garage, I'm not surprised that everything, as usual, is in its place. And her mom's Volvo is already there.

We go through the door that enters into the kitchen, and I can smell something baking combined with the smell of pine, which I assume is coming from the enormous Christmas tree in front of the big window in their great room.

"Hey, Mom," calls Olivia.

"In here," says her mom.

"Samantha's with me."

"Oh, good." Her mom steps around the corner and joins us in the kitchen. "I haven't seen you since before Thanksgiving, Samantha. How are you doing?"

"I'm okay. It sure smells good in here."

"I'm trying out this new five-minute fudge recipe I saw on TV," she says. "You guys will have to sample it after it sets."

"No problem," says Olivia.

"Your tree looks great," I tell her. "We don't even have one up yet."

She smiles. "Well, you know me. I have to get one up the first week of December. Will thinks I'm nuts. But it just puts me in the spirit. Did you girls hear that we're supposed to get snow tomorrow?"

"Cool," says Olivia.

"I thought it felt pretty cold today," I say. "I hope it doesn't put too much of a damper on the Christmas parade."

"That's right," says Mrs. Marsh. "I nearly forgot about it. Are you going to be Mrs. Santa again this year, Samantha?"

Olivia laughs. "No, she worked a deal with her mom."

"I'm doing Christmas cards instead."

"Your mom's lucky," she tells me, then looks at Olivia. "Any chance I can work a deal with you?"

"Maybe." Olivia grabs my arm and starts pulling me away. "Let me know what you have to offer, and I'll get back to you."

There have been times when I felt seriously jealous of Olivia's family. And back during my "dark era" after Dad died and I pushed God away, I almost let it come between my friendship with her. But for the most part, I think I've gotten over it. Mostly I'm thankful that I get to participate with her family. And really, they've been amazingly good to me. Still, I get twinges sometimes. Not really jealousy though. More like I wonder why Olivia's family seems to have it so good and my family struggles so much. It's one of those things I plan to ask God about when we're up in heaven. Although I suspect that I might not really care by then. But it's reassuring to know that I can ask if I want to.

We spend a fairly uneventful evening, and I'm relieved that my mom doesn't call me. We watch our movie, which is only so-so, play some computer games, eat too much fudge, then to compensate, do a workout in their mini-gym down in the basement. And finally we're both ready to call it a night.

"Are you worried about tomorrow?" Olivia asks after the lights are off and I'm almost drifting to sleep.

"A little."

"I'm sure it'll be fine."

And the next thing I know, it's morning, and since we overslept and it's already eight-thirty, we have to scramble to get dressed and out the door on time.

"What's the hurry?" Olivia's mom asks as we head toward the door to the garage. "I've got cinnamon rolls in the oven."

"Sounds great," I tell her. "But I have to, uh, be somewhere." I glance nervously at Olivia. She knows that I don't want anyone to know about my involvement in the case, or my "special gift." Including her parents.

"I promised to drop Sam at an appointment, but I'll be back in about twenty minutes."

"Okay. Well, see you later, Samantha," calls Mrs. Marsh.

"Bye. Thanks."

"This is going to be tricky," Olivia says as she starts her car.

"You mean not telling people?"

"Yeah. What if you end up helping to locate Kayla and then the newspaper gets ahold of this story? What will you do then?"

"I don't know. I just hope we can prevent that. I'll ask Ebony."

Olivia drops me off in front of the precinct, telling me to call when I need a ride. And this time when I go up the steps, I don't get the same sense that Dad is there. But I imagine he is. I imagine that he's watching me. And smiling.

"There you are," Ebony says when I peek into her office.

"Sorry I'm a little late."

"No problem. Michael just got here too. He's just getting set up down the hall. I'll show you where."

"Hey, Michelangelo," calls Ebony. "Here's our girl."

"Almost ready," says a short, stocky man with a gray beard and a ponytail. He's wearing an oversized corduroy shirt about the color of an eggplant, and when he smiles, a gold front tooth flashes in the overhead fluorescent light.

"This is Samantha McGregor," says Ebony. "And this is Michael Taylor, the renowned composite artist."

We shake hands, and he holds on to mine for just a few seconds longer than necessary, but he's kind of squinting and has this thoughtful look on his face. "I sense that Samantha has a very deep spirit," he finally says as he releases my hand. "I think I will enjoy working with her."

"I hope so," I say nervously.

"Ebony showed me your answers to my questions." He pulls out a chair for me. "It gives us a place to start."

"Do you mind if I sit in?" asks Ebony.

He seems to consider this. "As long as you don't interrupt. I can't abide interruptions. It messes with the waves."

"The waves?" I question.

"Yes. I rely on intuition as much as anything else. Surely you understand that, Samantha."

I glance at Ebony. "Did you tell him about me?"

She nods. "I needed to let him know that you hadn't actually *seen* the suspect. Not physically anyway."

"No worries," he tells me. "I understand these things. You can trust me, Samantha."

"It's just that I don't really want other people to know about this," I explain to both of them. "I mean, it's hard for some people to understand this. And I'd rather just keep it under wraps, you know?"

Michael nods. "Oh, believe me, I know." He makes a zipping gesture across his mouth. "These lips are sealed."

"Mine too," says Ebony.

So we settle into this thing. First Michael encourages me to just relax, and he chats about pretty much nothing for a while. Then after a few minutes, he asks me to close my eyes and to focus on the image I saw yesterday. Then he starts to ask me more questions. But it's not so much about what I saw as about how it made me feel.

And then he asks about the apron and the kinds of letters that spelled out the name Colby. He asks me about colors and shapes, and then he goes into more details about the actual facial description. And it's weird because I can't imagine how some of his questions would really help him, but I try not to think about that. I just try to answer them, the best I can. Then after about an hour, he tells me to open my eyes.

"Now, I'm going to let you see what I've drawn, Samantha, but I want you to know that it's only the beginning. I'm sure it won't look like the man you saw in your vision. Not completely anyway. But we'll find the features that are right, and we'll try to adjust the parts that aren't." He smiles, and that gold tooth glints in the light again. "You ready?"

I nod.

He turns his large sketch pad around for me to see, and I am shocked that it actually feels very familiar—and creepy. "Wow," I say quietly, getting out of my chair to see it better.

"Are we closer than I thought?"

The drawing shows a man from the waist up, clearly depicting the apron and name Colby on the right side. He has a rounded face, somewhat coarse-looking features, a stubble beard, and a receding hair-line. But it's the small piercing eyes that get me. I make a face. "He gives me the heebie-jeebies."

"Not exactly the kind of guy who someone like Kayla would be attracted to?" asks Ebony.

"Not at all. He looks like the kind of person Kayla would make fun of. Like some old, geeky geezer dude who pumps gas and hits on high school girls for kicks."

Then I point out some things that don't seem quite right, and Michael changes his eyebrows and puts his eyes farther apart, broadens his nose, and narrows his lips. After about an hour, I am pretty satisfied.

"I mean, it's hard to say for sure," I admit. "When I see something in a vision, it's so fast, and some of it doesn't even feel visual, you know? But I really think that looks a lot like the guy I saw."

"Works for me," Ebony says as Michael hands her the final drawing. "I plan to run it today." She shakes Michael's hand. "You do good work, Michael."

"I hope it helps to catch the jerk," he says. Then he turns to me. "Of course, I couldn't have done it without Samantha." He smiles. "You've got good instincts. If you have any artistic ability, you might be good at this."

I laugh. "Maybe I should show you my mountains."

"Mountains?"

Then Ebony explains.

"Well, I don't usually do landscapes, but maybe I should take a look," he offers. "Maybe I could help to make it look more like the real deal."

I pull out my very amateurish-looking drawing, and he nods. "Yep. Looks like Arizona to me." Then he gets out a fresh piece of paper and starts drawing. Within minutes he's taken what look like a five-year-old's squiggles and turned them into something that might be real. I point out a couple of things that I remembered differently.

"Like this shape." I point to my drawing. "It was kind of like a bear's head. Or maybe a monkey head. I mean, the profile."

So he starts playing with it some more.

"Yes," I tell him when he gets it right. "Like that!"

Finally he's done, and I feel like it's similar to what I envisioned.

"This could be very helpful," says Ebony. "It's obviously a long shot, but you never know. Anyway, I'll see if I can find someone who knows Arizona geography well enough to identify this location."

I stare at Michael's landscape and wonder about Arizona. I've never been there before, and I try to imagine Kayla there now. What is she doing right this moment? What is she thinking? Is she frightened or sorry or even alive?

After we tell Michael good-bye, Ebony walks me down the hallway, pausing in front of her office. I can tell something's bugging her. "You have a minute, Samantha?"

"Sure."

"Come in."

I follow her in, and she closes the door. "I talked to your mom." She leans against her desk. "Did she mention anything to you?"

"Actually, I spent the night at Olivia's last night. I haven't talked to my mom yet."

"It did sound as if she's pretty busy right now, what with the parade today and then the winter carnival program that the park district runs for school-age kids during Christmas break. I'm sure her hands are more than full this time of year."

I nod. Of course, I want to add that they're always full—winter, spring, summer, or fall. Her job seems to consume her. But I don't say this.

"Well, she was very polite when I told her about what you're doing..."

"But...?"

"But she was concerned. She told me about sending

114

you to a counselor last year, and how she felt your grief for your dad was affecting you, well, in unusual ways."

"Like I was going off the deep end spiritually?"

She nods. "Something like that."

"It makes her uncomfortable."

"I know."

"She thinks I'm crazy."

"I'm not sure that's it, exactly...but she doesn't really understand."

"So, what am I supposed to do?" I feel slightly desperate. "Pretend that I don't have these dreams or visions? It's not like I asked for this *gift*, you know. But am I supposed to turn my back on it? What about this thing with Kayla now? Do I just shut it down, ignore any more clues?"

Ebony frowns.

"I mean, you don't think I'm crazy, do you? You seem to take me seriously."

"Of course, I do." She smiles now. "I think you're an amazing girl, Samantha. And with your help, I think we might have a much better chance of finding Kayla."

"So, what do I do about my mom?"

"Just talk to her. Be honest, but try to understand how she feels too."

"How *does* she feel?"

Ebony's brow creases. "Scared."

"Scared?" I try to grasp this. My mom, the woman who can storm through our house venting her anger about Zach's irresponsibility, or who flips out over the fact that someone put the milk back in the fridge with only a few

drops in it? This woman who sometimes scares me is afraid? It's hard to swallow.

"I know that kids don't like to think of parents like that, Samantha. Parents are supposed to be brave and grown up—they're supposed to have the answers. Maybe I shouldn't have said what I did..."

"No, it's okay. But why? Why do you think she's scared?"

"Partly because her husband got killed—and on the job too. And she feels like it's all up to her now, to raise you kids—"

"We're practically grown-ups."

"Well, Zach may be going on twenty, but he's still not grown up yet. And your mom worries about you too, Samantha. And with the stress of her job, she's got a lot to deal with."

"Yeah," I admit. "I know you're right. And I try to do what I can to lighten her load. I'm pretty independent, and I stay out of trouble."

Ebony smiles. "I think you must be a mom's dream come true."

"Well, I wouldn't say that..."

"Hey, you should've seen me at your age." She leans her head back and laughs. "I was a mess."

"That's hard to believe."

"It's true. My poor mother. She'd just been widowed, and then it looked like I was going straight to the dogs. I think that was the year her hair turned completely gray. She has me to thank for that."

"But you turned out fine."

"Well, thank you."

"So, what should I do about my mom, Ebony? I mean, if she doesn't want me to be involved in this thing with Kayla?"

She shrugs. "I don't know that there's much you can do about that. She's your mom."

"Did she have to sign off on anything today?"

"Not officially. Because you won't be legally involved in the case. If there is a case, which remains to be seen, you won't be expected to testify since you're not an actual witness…so we should be okay. But it did make me feel better to have her verbal consent for you to come here today."

"So, do you think I need permission for anything else like this?" I ask. "I mean, do you think I should tell her if something else comes up? Like if I have another dream about Kayla or something? Should I ask her permission to talk to you?"

"I don't know, but I do think you should *talk* to her. Just clear the air and hopefully come to some kind of an understanding. Ask her what she'd like you to do under those circumstances. In some ways she seems like a fairly laid-back mom. It sounds like she lets you come and go. I'm sure it's because she really trusts you."

"Yeah. Or maybe she just doesn't have the time to deal with me."

"She's fortunate that you're a good girl, Samantha. It really does give her one less thing to worry about."

"So she told you about Zach then?" I feel worried about this. After all, Ebony is a policewoman, and Zach has been known to break the law occasionally. If she knew something specifically, would Ebony have a responsibility to arrest him? Could my relationship with Ebony get my brother in serious trouble? Would he blame me?

"She told me a little about him. We actually had a really nice conversation, Samantha. I feel for your mom. And because of working with your dad, and now with you, well, I feel a kind of connection to your family. I know that Zach is going through some hard stuff right now. And like I said, I was a wild child myself—the daughter of a good-hearted preacher man who brought shame to her family. I know how it feels to struggle like that, how it feels to be lost and confused. I can relate to Zach."

I sigh. "That's good to know."

"But you know what I think?"

"No."

"I think God is at work in your family, and even if it doesn't look too great right now, I think it's going to get better."

I force a little smile. "I hope so."

"Talk to your mom, okay?"

"Okay."

I thank Ebony for her little pep talk, and then as I'm leaving the precinct, I notice that the holding area for the Christmas parade is starting to fill up. Floats and cars and horses and things are getting into place behind city hall. I'm pretty sure that my mom will be over there now, probably doing some last-minute things on the park district float. How it looks is a direct reflection on her.

And suddenly I know what I need to do. I call Olivia on my cell phone. "I guess I don't need a ride after all."

"Why not? Did something go wrong?"

"No, not at all. In fact, it went really well. The artist was amazing. I'll call you back later and fill you in on the whole thing. I've just decided to head over to see if my mom needs any help on the parade."

"Watch out," she warns me. "You might get stuck putting on that old Mrs. Santa suit again."

"Nah, I think they're doing some kind of a barnyard theme this year. Maybe they'll need a cow."

She laughs. "Call me."

As I walk over to the holding area, a few snowflakes start to fall. I look up, and the sky seems lower, and it's gray and heavy looking. This should get the kids hyped up. A Christmas parade *and* snow!

I spot the park district float over by where the high school marching band is assembling. I wave at a couple of friends who play in the band, then go over to where I find my mom assisting one of the day care kids who's dressed as a pig. The elastic string on his snout is too loose, and instead of a nose, it looks like a chin.

"Hey, Mom," I call out as I join her. "Need a hand with anything?"

She looks surprised. "Does this mean you're bailing on my Christmas cards?"

"No, I'm just trying to share a little Christmas cheer."

"See if you can make this stay on Benjie for me." She hands me the rubber pig snout. "This is my daughter," she tells the boy. "Her name is Samantha."

"You're pretty," says the boy.

"Thanks." I shorten the elastic by tying a knot in the back. "You're pretty cute for a pig."

He laughs. "I'm not really a pig."

"I know." I put the snout back on him. "How's that?"

He makes a snorting sound, which I suppose means it's okay.

After that, I become my mom's right-hand girl, running around and helping kids with costume adjustments, nose wiping, and restapling the sign that's starting to fall off. Then we're lifting the kids onto the float and arranging them amid the straw bales and fence posts that are supposed to keep them from falling off. And then finally there's no more time, and whether or not they're ready, my mom announces that it's time to take off.

"Break a leg!" she yells as they start to roll. "But don't let any of them fall off," she says more quietly.

"Don't worry." Kellie, one of the day care teachers, waves. She's dressed as a farmer. "We'll be fine."

Then Mom turns to me and lets out a big sigh. "You hungry?"

"You mean you're not going to watch the parade?"

She laughs in a sarcastic way. "Are you kidding? It's freezing out here." Then she looks up. "And it's snowing! Let's go find a warm place and get something to eat."

Once we're in her car, she's trying to think of a restaurant. "All my regular favorites are on the parade route. And with this weather, they'll probably be packed with people taking refuge." She turns to me. "Any ideas?"

"How about Rosie's?"

"Rosie's?" Her brow creases in a frown.

"Yeah. I was there last week, and it was good."

She slowly nods. "Okay, then Rosie's it is. At least they shouldn't be very busy."

As we walk into the deli, I know what Mom is thinking. I don't mean in a psychic kind of way either. I know because I'm sure it's the same thing I was thinking when I came here with Ebony. Mom's remembering Dad, remembering how he liked to come here. But maybe that's a good thing. Maybe it will make it easier to talk to her. And I have a strong feeling (also not psychic) that's why we're here. To talk.

We place our orders, and taking our hot drinks with us, we go to sit down. I send up a silent prayer, asking God to help this conversation. It seems like we could be off to a good start, but I know my mom—it could easily turn sideways. However, I think it's in my favor that we're in a public place right now. She can't get too aggravated with others looking on. Not that this place is busy. Other than the deli workers and an elderly couple, the place is deserted. Still, my mom doesn't like making a scene.

"I had a nice long chat with Ebony Hamilton last night."

"Uh-huh." I spoon the whipped cream off my hot cocoa.

"She says you're helping her to find Kayla Henderson." I can hear a trace of sarcasm in her voice, like she still finds this pretty hard to believe.

I slowly nod as I blow across the top of my cup.

"She said that you've had several visions about Kayla." Her voice is getting that slight hard edge to it now. I can tell she's getting irritated.

I take in a deep breath. "That's right, Mom. I have. And it's not like I wanted to. They just came, okay? They seem to be clues, like God is trying to show me where Kayla is—and that she needs help."

"I thought she just ran off with a boy."

"That's what a lot of people thought. But that might not be the case."

"They said she was seen boarding a bus, Samantha. Of her own free will. No one was forcing her to leave town."

"I know."

"But you've had these visions?" Her words are coated with skepticism, and it hurts.

"Yeah…" I look down at my cocoa and silently ask God to help me. I want to say something mean back to her, but that won't help. I try to remember what Ebony told me—*just talk to her.* Help her to understand.

"It doesn't make sense, Samantha. Why would God give you visions?"

"Why not? God is God. He can do what He wants."

She rolls her eyes. "Believe me, *I know.*"

"Look, Mom, I didn't ask for this, but I know that it's real. And Ebony told me about Grandma McGregor and how she was like that too."

"Ebony knew about Grandma McGregor?" Mom looks shocked now.

"Dad told her. Back when they were partners. I guess he told her a little about me too."

Mom looks sad as she sips her coffee.

"Do you mind if I keep helping her? I mean, if God gives me any more dreams or visions about Kayla—would it bother you if I stayed involved with the case?"

"It seems crazy, Samantha."

"I know...sometimes I think it's crazy too. But at the same time, I know it's a gift from God. Dad was the first one to tell me that. Remember?"

"I remember. Not that I agreed. I just kept quiet because I didn't know what else to do." She sets her cup down and looks directly at me. "I just don't want you getting in over your head, Samantha. You're only sixteen. And I don't understand why God would give a gift like this to someone so young. Or why He'd give it to anyone for that matter. It doesn't make sense."

"Maybe it's to show that He's God," I say, not mentioning that I'm not "only sixteen," but soon to be seventeen. Although I'm sure that's not her point. Instead I try to make mine. "Maybe He wants to remind us that He's all-powerful and all-knowing—and that He cares about us."

"It just seems very weird."

"If you read the Bible, you'll see that there are lots of things that seem very weird."

"Well, it makes me uncomfortable."

"God makes people uncomfortable sometimes."

Our food comes now, and we both use this as an excuse to take a break from the discussion. Finally, Mom breaks the silence.

"This is good." She holds up her partially eaten sandwich. "I forgot that I liked the food here so much."

"Yeah. Me too."

"Here's the deal, Samantha. If you really believe this thing—this *gift*—is from God…well, I guess I can't really argue with you on it. But if I begin to notice any strange behavior, anything that causes me to be concerned, then I'm going to ask you to see Paula again."

"I can live with that."

"As far as working with Ebony…well, she seems like a levelheaded person. I suppose I can trust her. But I'm going to give her the same warning. If you start acting weird, start going off the deep end, I expect her to notify me."

"I'm sure she would anyway."

"So, we agree then?"

"Totally."

"Okay." Mom shrugs. "Though I can't imagine how it's going to do any good."

"If it makes you feel any better, I don't talk about this to anyone. Besides Olivia and, of course, Ebony. It's not like I want people to know about it. I know they would think it's weird."

She nods. "You're right about that. And I appreciate it. I don't want people at work asking me about my psychic daughter."

"I'm not a psychic, Mom."

"I know that, Samantha. But other people might think you are."

And then she changes the subject to Zach and how she's worried that he's getting into drugs again. "There was a message on the machine last night. The video store called to let him know that he's fired." She sighs. "Big surprise there."

"I suspected as much."

Her brow creases. "You had a vision?"

"No." I sort of laugh. "Olivia and I were at the video store last night, and they seemed pretty ticked that he hadn't come to work."

"Oh." She frowns. "Well, if you really are gifted in *seeing* things, Samantha, why doesn't God use this gift to help your own family? Why don't you ask God to show you some way to fix Zach?"

"I wish it were that simple, Mom." I suppress my irritation. "It's not like I can control it. It's something that God does. I just try to be available."

Mom glances at her watch. "Speaking of being available, I should probably head back to the parade to make sure it went okay. You ready?"

As Mom drives back toward town, I feel a small sense of relief. At least she seems signed off on me working with Ebony. Still, I feel sad too. I know that Mom doesn't believe in this gift. I know that she thinks I'm just playing some kind of bizarre game. Like maybe I need to act like this "crazy girl" to get attention. And the truth is exactly the opposite. As much as I want to serve God, as much as I want to help Kayla, my life would be much simpler without this kind of gift. I just hope God really knows what He's doing.

Twelve

Looks like we haven't missed much." Mom parks her car back in the reserved section of the holding area. The last participants in the parade, including Santa's sleigh, are just heading out now. "They must've had some delays along the way."

"I think I'll call Olivia to come and pick me up," I tell Mom as we get out of her car.

"You don't want to see the end of the parade? Or sit on Santa's lap?" she teases as we walk across the parking lot toward Main Street.

"Tempting as that sounds, I think I'll pass." I pull out my new phone and flip it open.

She looks at my phone. "Pretty fancy. Ebony must really be taking you seriously."

"I guess..."

"Or else she's trying to make up for something."

I look curiously at my mom. "What do you mean?"

"Maybe she feels guilty, Samantha."

"For what?"

"You know..." Mom begins to walk faster, and I hurry to keep pace with her.

"No, I don't know. What?"

"She was with your dad that day. She was his partner. Maybe she feels guilty."

"No," I say quickly since we're around other people now. "That's not it."

"You just never know, Samantha…" She gives me this look now. Kind of dark and foreboding and suspicious looking. And I can't believe this woman is really my mom.

"See you later." I turn in the other direction, feeling like I can't get away from her fast enough. And okay, I know the Bible says to respect your parents, but it's hard to respect that.

I dial Olivia's number, but her cell is turned off. So I call her house and get the answering machine. Great! Now I'm stuck in town. I glance over at what I'm guessing is getting close to the end of the parade coming around the corner and entering Main Street. The group of horses and soggy riders slog their way through the slushy snow. It seems to be melting as quickly as it falls. Even so, it's biting cold out here, and I'm sure that Mom won't be heading home for hours. Not that I want to ride with her.

I duck into Lava Java Coffee House which, of course, is packed. But at least it's warm in here. I get into the line, trying to decide what to do next. As I'm standing there, I'm thinking, why doesn't God show me what to do at times like this? And if I really were a psychic, which I'm not, wouldn't I have known that Olivia wouldn't be able to pick me up? Wouldn't I have come up with some kind of backup plan?

"Samantha," a guy says, and I turn to see Conrad Stiles rubbing his hands together as he steps into line behind me. "I thought that looked like you."

"Hey, Conrad." Suddenly I feel very self-conscious, and I remember every word Olivia said about how Conrad's been asking about me. I wonder if he knows what I'm thinking?

"How's it going?"

I shrug. "I was freezing out there, so I thought I'd get something to warm up with."

"Me too."

"Did you come to watch the parade?" That's kind of weird, but you never know.

He grins. "Not exactly. I'm supposed to pick up my little sister, Katie. She's marching with the *Amazing Mini Majorettes*."

"The little girls who twirl batons?"

He nods. "Pretty hokey, huh?"

"I think they're cute." I move up a few inches in the line, and he follows. "In fact, I remember how I wanted to be a twirler when I was a little girl."

"How come you didn't?"

"Well, the only time I really wanted to do it was during the parades, and that was only because I thought their costumes were cool. After that, I'd forget all about it. Besides, I'm kind of a klutz. I probably would've dropped my baton too much or seriously injured someone."

He laughs. "So, what are you doing here? Did you come to watch the parade?"

"I was helping my mom with the park district float," I tell him, which isn't untrue. "It gets pretty crazy with all the little kids right before the parade starts."

We continue chatting like this as the line makes a snail pace forward, and finally I am ordering a coffee. I decide to get a mocha.

"Want to sit together?" Conrad asks as I move out of the line to wait for my drink.

"Sure."

"Why don't you find a spot, and I'll bring your coffee with mine."

So I hand him my receipt and go off in search of a table. The place is packed, but just as I get to the back of the room, a couple of women vacate their little round table, and I pounce on it. I unzip my coat and loosen my scarf then dig into my backpack until I find my lip gloss, which I quickly apply.

Okay, I don't normally consider myself a vain person, but there's nothing wrong with caring a little. Of course, this makes me wonder how my hair is doing, but based on this damp, snowy weather, I can be fairly certain that it's probably frizzing all over the place by now. Oh, the blessing of these natural curls.

Olivia is always telling me that she'd happily trade hair with me, which I think is nuts since she has the most gor-geous long blond hair that's naturally straight and silky. Of course, her complaint is that she has to wash it every single day to look decent. Whereas my hair is really low maintenance. I can go several days without a shampoo—

maybe even a week if I was camping. So I guess I should be thankful.

"You found a table." Conrad sets our coffees down then removes his damp letterman's jacket, gives it a shake, and hangs it over the back of his chair. Then he pulls off his wool knit cap, which causes his hair to stick out in absolutely every direction.

I can't help but chuckle, but I try to cover it up by taking a quick sip of my mocha.

"Yeah, I know." He sits down. "I probably look like Bozo the Clown now. It's bad enough having red hair, but I'll bet it looks like something exploded up there." He gives it a pat, which only manages to flatten the top so he really does look like Bozo.

"I don't think that's going to help much. But hey, if it makes you feel better, I sort of know how you feel." I do the little hand plumping motion to the side of my own hair. "I'm sure my lovely locks are looking pretty wild too."

"I *like* your hair."

I sort of nod, unsure of how to react to this unexpected compliment. Olivia is always telling me that I'm not good with flattery—probably because I seldom hear it. "Well, thanks," I finally mutter. "I think that curls are kind of an acquired taste."

"I happen to think straight hair is boring."

I laugh. "I guess I never thought of it like that."

"Maybe you should."

"So how do you know when to pick up your little sister?"

He takes his cell phone out of his pocket then sets it on the table. "She's supposed to call when they're done."

"She has her own cell phone?"

He laughs. "She wishes. But Katie's like six years old. She's borrowing my mom's. Both my parents had to work today. That's why I'm on Katie patrol."

"So, did you watch her in the parade?"

"Yeah, of course." He takes a sip of his coffee. It looks like a mocha too. That's nice.

"Did she drop her baton?"

"Not that I saw. But then, she still had a long ways to go too."

"Man, I bet they're freezing their little legs off today, if they're wearing those short outfits, that is."

He nods. "Yeah, they looked pretty chilly. But at least they're moving."

We chat for a while, and I'm surprised at how easy it is to talk to him. He seems like just a regular guy. And I suppose he is. But he's also a fairly cool guy around our school. Or so I've imagined. The truth is, I don't really know Conrad very well. Mostly that he's a Christian and that he's involved in a lot of sports and school activities. But we haven't really traveled in the same circle much. Did Olivia really tell him the things we talked about last week? Suddenly I hope not.

I glance at the empty street outside and then down at my watch. "Looks like the parade's over. I'm surprised your sister hasn't called yet."

A frown creases his forehead. "Yeah, me too."

And just as he says this, I experience one of those flashes and in the same instant I see a little red-haired girl wearing a purple majorette outfit, and she's crying.

"Are you okay?" he asks me.

I blink then nod, still trying to take in what I just witnessed. I feel certain that it was Katie but equally certain that I can't just blurt that information out. Like how crazy would that sound?

"I think we should go look for your sister." I suddenly stand up and grab my coat, and without waiting for him, I press through the crowded room, making my way for the door.

"Hey, wait," he calls, but I keep going.

As I walk down the congested sidewalk, I try to remember what else I saw just now. What was it that Katie was standing in front of? But it seemed like it was just some trees. Ghostlike white tree trunks. And here we are in the middle of town where the only trees are the cone-shaped evergreens planted in the big pots on each corner. Then it hits me—it had to be the birch trees at the city park.

"Where are you going?" asks Conrad.

"To the park."

"Why?"

"Isn't that where you're supposed to pick up the kids after the parade?" I hope that this might somehow make sense. Or at least sounds believable. Although I know it must sound nuts.

"I don't know…"

"Well, I do. My mom works for the park district, and I'm sure that's where Katie is right now." Okay, even nuttier. But I don't have time to worry about this. I know that Katie needs us—now.

"I'm going to call her." Conrad opens his cell phone. But as he dials, he keeps pace with me. And I continue walking as fast as I can.

I turn and glance at him, wondering if Katie is going to answer the phone. If she's going to say that she's perfectly fine and waiting for him to come get her on the other end of town. Even so, I keep walking toward the park.

"The phone's turned off," he tells me.

Finally we're at the city park, which is mostly deserted, but there standing right in front of those very birch trees is the same little red-haired girl with tears running down both cheeks.

"Katie!" Conrad jogs over and picks her up, wrapping his coat around her. "What are you doing here?"

"I got lost." Then she buries her head into his shoulder and cries even harder. I'm standing by the two of them now, not sure of what I should do. Maybe just pull a vanishing act and hope that he forgets my involvement in this.

"Katie?" he says in a gentle voice, "why didn't you just call me on Mom's phone like we'd planned?"

"I lost Mom's phone!" Now she cries even harder. "It was clipped to my boot, just like you told me. It must've come off when we were marching. Mom's going to be so mad at me."

"It's okay, Katie," he says in a soothing tone. "Mom won't be mad. She'll be glad that you're okay. How'd you get lost anyway?"

"I was trying to find Mom's phone. I thought I would go back and see if it was in the street, and then I couldn't find Claudia or the other girls, and I didn't know which way to go. And I'm not supposed to talk to strangers." She's starting to cry again.

"I better go," I say quietly, glancing over my shoulder like I have someplace I should be right now.

"Need a lift?" he offers with an apologetic smile.

I consider this. "Well, sort of..."

"My car's parked over by The Pet Place."

Conrad continues to carry Katie as we walk about six blocks to The Pet Place. By the time we get there, she seems mostly calmed down, but she's still worried about losing her mom's phone.

"We should go look for it, Conrad," she tells him as he sets her down beside an odd-looking older car that's the color of a ripe tangerine.

He frowns as he opens the passenger door and pulls the front seat forward so she can climb into the back. "I don't think we can find it, Katie. Maybe someone else will. We'll try calling Mom's number again later to see if it's been turned in somewhere. Don't worry. Just buckle your seat belt and wrap up in that blanket before you catch pneumonia."

Then he flops the front seat back into place for me. "Sorry about all this."

"You don't need to be sorry about anything," I tell him. "Just be glad you found her."

He nods then peers at me curiously. "But how did you know she was in the park?"

I shrug, imitating his surprised expression. "Just a weird hunch, I guess."

I get into the car, and as Conrad walks around, Katie asks, "Who are you anyway?"

I turn around and smile at her. "Sorry, Katie. We didn't really meet, did we? I'm Samantha."

"Are you Conrad's girlfriend?" she asks in a slightly teasing tone as Conrad gets in.

I laugh. "No. We're just friends."

"Samantha helped me to find you," he tells her as he starts the car.

"How?" asks Katie.

"I just had a feeling—I think it was a God-thing." And before anyone can question me further, I change the subject. "So, other than getting lost, how was the parade today?"

"It was okay."

"Did you drop your baton at all?" I ask.

"Yeah…but only twice."

"So, what do you do when that happens?"

"You pick it up," she says in this "duh" voice.

I laugh. "Yeah, well, that makes sense. But is it hard to get back into formation with the other girls after you pick it up? And do you feel embarrassed for dropping it?"

"Well, Claudia—that's our coach—says not to feel bad. She says that everyone drops the baton sometimes.

The thing is to just get back in line and keep going. And not to think about it. I mean, dropping the baton."

"Claudia sounds really smart," I tell her.

"I guess…" She lets out a loud sigh. "And besides Mary Grace dropped her baton way more than me. She dropped it about a hundred times."

"The old comparison game." Conrad winks at me. "Starts a lot younger than you'd think, huh?"

Then I tell him where I live, and the car gets quiet. I'm worried that he might still be wondering how I knew where to find his sister. "What kind of car is this anyway?" I ask, hoping to keep us focused in a different direction.

He laughs. "You really want to know?"

"Yeah. I don't think I've ever seen one like it. What is it called anyway?"

"It's a Gremlin."

"Really? That's what it's called? A Gremlin?"

"Yep. A 1976 Gremlin, made by American Motors. My mom talked my dad into getting it for her a couple years ago. She used to have one just like it back when she was my age. She said she was going to drive it herself, but then she decided it wasn't quite as comfy as her Acura."

"So you got it?"

"Yeah. My dad doesn't want to sell it unless he can get what he paid back for it." He laughs. "Like that's going to happen in this century."

"Well, I think it's kind of cool. And it even goes with your hair."

Now he laughs even harder. "Yeah, figures you would notice that."

Then we're at my house, and I thank Conrad for the ride and tell Katie good-bye and that I hope they find her mom's phone. I get out, but I've only taken a few steps away from the car when I realize that Conrad is right behind me. Suddenly I'm worried that he's going to ask me about finding Katie again, and how did I know she was lost, and how did I know where to find her. Maybe he'll even be like my old neighbor after I found his guinea pig; maybe Conrad will accuse me of setting this whole thing up just to get his attention. I brace myself.

"Uh, Samantha. Do you think you'd want to go out with me sometime?"

"Huh?" Okay, that was a totally stupid response. But it's too late to undo it.

"Just as friends, you know. I mean, I know that you're not really into dating too much. Olivia explained how you need to get to know a guy as a friend and everything before you really want to date or anything. And I'm cool with that. Really, I'd just like to get to know you better."

"Oh." I nod. "Sure, that sounds cool."

"I thought maybe we could even invite someone else to come along, if you'd like that, I mean. Maybe Alex and Olivia. Do you think Olivia would be up for something like that?"

I try not to grin. "I don't know," I say in a totally calm voice. "But I can ask her and see."

"Not as a double date," he says quickly. "Don't tell her that."

"Okay."

"Can I call you then?"

"Sure." Then I give him my cell phone number. But as soon as I say it, I wonder if that's a mistake. This phone is supposed to be for official use, at least for the most part. So I give him my home phone too. "I don't always have my cell on."

"Okay, see ya around then."

"See ya."

As soon as I'm in the house, I call Olivia on the land line, and I tell her everything.

"That's awesome, Samantha!"

"Yeah, can you believe it?"

"It's almost like God wanted to get you guys together."

"Oh, I don't know about that…"

"But what about your vision about Katie? Why would God do that?"

"Because she needed help?" I'm thinking, *Like duh*, but I don't say it.

"But because she needed help, you got to spend time with Conrad," she says as if that proves something.

"Maybe that's all this was…" Realization is hitting me now. "Seriously, I bet the only reason I spent any time with Conrad was only so God could show me that Katie needed help. That's probably all there was to it. And maybe Conrad won't even call me. Maybe it was just his way of—"

"Maybe you should just wait and see!" interrupts Olivia. "Good grief, you don't have to second-guess every single thing, Samantha."

I kind of laugh. "Yeah, I know."

But the truth is, I am sort of driven to figure things out. And I don't think it's just because of my "gift" either. I just think it's this curious part of my nature that makes me want to understand everything about everything, and it's hard to turn it off. Although I know it can irritate some people. Like it used to make my parents nuts when I'd ask *why* about every little thing. And it bugs Olivia when I start to question things like I did just now. And sometimes it even gets to me. Like I have to tell myself to *just chill*. Lighten up! Still, I guess that's just how God made me. And someday I'm sure I'll find out all the reasons why.

Thirteen

When I come downstairs, I'm surprised to find Zach home. He's standing in front of the refrigerator and just staring.

"Cooling off the kitchen?" I pick up his coat from the floor and hang it over the back of a chair.

"Huh?" He turns and looks at me with this totally blank expression that isn't a bit reassuring. Then he pulls out the carton of milk and closes the door.

"Where's your car? I didn't see it in the driveway when I got home."

"Don't ask."

"Why?"

"Because my car is no more." He pours a glass of milk, then begins to peruse through the pantry until he finds a box of Vanilla Wafers.

"No more?"

"Yeah, as in totaled."

"Did you get in a wreck?"

"Sort of…" He sits down at the island and digs into the half-full box.

"Did you get hurt?"

"Not really."

"Did anyone else get hurt?"

"No. It was just me." He looks up and kind of smiles, but his eyes have this blank expression. "Just me and my car...and then it was just me." He sort of laughs, but it doesn't sound cheery. "Just me and my feet."

"What happened, Zach?" I sit across from him and reach for the box. He frowns as I take out a couple of cookies. "I think there's enough to go around," I assure him. "But seriously, what happened to your car? I mean, where is it?"

"Where is it?" He just shakes his head.

"You mean you don't know where your car is, Zach?"

"Oh, I sort of know... I'm just not too sure."

"Are you high?"

"High?" He looks all around him now, like he's trying to figure it out.

"You are, aren't you?"

He looks down at the floor. "Well, I'm about three feet off the ground. I guess if you call that high—"

"You know what I mean, Zach!" I glare at him now. "You're on something, aren't you? And that's why you didn't go to work last night, why you lost your job and wrecked your—"

"Whaddya mean I lost my job?" He actually looks surprised by this news.

"Listen to the message machine. Mom said they called."

"I got fired just because I was in a wreck?"

"You got fired because you didn't show up for work. And because it's not the first time."

Then he lets loose with some off-color language.

"You feel better now?"

He frowns. "No."

"You need help, Zach."

"I need my ——- job back!" He snaps at me and grabs the box of cookies.

"Hey, it's not my fault."

"It's not my fault either."

"How can you say that?"

"I told you, I got in a wreck. I had to walk back to town. How was I supposed to go to work?"

"You could've called someone."

"With what?"

"So, where did you go after you got back to town?" I ask. "Mom said you never came home last night."

"I stayed with a friend."

"And why were you driving around anyway?"

"It's a free country," he says. "I can drive if I want to."

"You could," I remind him. "You can't now."

Ignoring me, he tips the box up and pours the last of the crumbs into his mouth then washes that down with his milk.

"So, how are you going to get your car? Does it need to be towed?"

He nods then wipes his mouth with the grimy-looking sleeve of his plaid flannel shirt. I look at him more closely; he's in serious need of a shower and clean clothes right now. "You look like you slept in a ditch last night. Although I'm sure you would've frozen if you had."

"You sound just like Mom, Samantha. Nag, nag, nag."

"Maybe it's because we care about you, Zach. Maybe it's because we're worried."

"Well, don't be. I can take care of myself."

I nod. "Yeah, it sure looks like it."

He stands up now and, leaving his mess behind, goes for the phone. He takes it around the corner, but not so far away that I can't hear. Now, I don't really like to eavesdrop, but the truth is, I'm getting seriously worried about Zach. I feel certain that he's on something. And that can only mean trouble.

"No way!" he says loudly enough that I don't have to strain my ears to hear. Then he cusses, and I can tell he's infuriated about something. "No stinking way, man! They can't do that. It's my car!" Then there's a brief silence, and Zach cusses again. "Are you positive about this? You know for sure they took it?" He groans. "What am I gonna do, man? I'm fried."

When he returns the phone to its cradle in the kitchen, I pretend to be busy loading the dishwasher. "Something wrong?"

"No!" he snarls, hitting his fist on the counter. "*Everything's* wrong!"

I make my face look as concerned as I can, hoping to appear more empathetic than I feel. The truth is, I'd like to knock my brother in the head right now. I can't believe that he's such a mess. "Anything I can help with?"

"Yeah, right."

"Is it about your car?" I ask, knowing full well that it is.

"Yeah." He cusses again. "The stupid police towed it away."

"The police?"

"Yeah. It's impounded."

"But how do you know that? I mean, how do you know it was the police? Don't they usually just put a sticker on your car, give you a few days before—"

"Yeah, that's what you'd think. But not for me...no, I'm the lucky one. I get the stinking police to impound my car." And now, to my total shock, he begins to cry.

"Zach? What's wrong? I mean, I know it's lousy to lose your car, but it's not the end of—"

"It's the end of me." He looks at me with frightened eyes.

"But why?"

"Because I'm stupid." He slams his fist into the counter again, so hard I almost expect to see a hole or broken bones. "I'm such a screwup, Samantha. I'm a mess."

"What is it, Zach?" I plead with him. "I mean, I know you're probably on something right now, but you can go back to rehab, maybe stay in longer this time and make sure—"

"That's not it." He leans over onto the counter. "I was carrying something—something in my car, you know, for a friend."

"Carrying something?"

"You know...*something* I shouldn't have. But it wasn't mine, Samantha. I swear it wasn't mine. I was just doing a friend a favor."

"You were transporting drugs in your car, Zach?"

He nods and breaks down into tears. "What am I gonna do? The cops have my car. They probably have the stuff. They're probably on their way—"

"Turn yourself in."

"What?" He looks at me like I've lost my mind.

"It's the smartest thing to do."

"No way."

"It is. Listen to me. If you turn yourself in and if you tell them the truth—"

"I can't!"

"You have to, Zach."

"They'll lock me up."

"Maybe they will," I admit. "But it won't be for as long. I'm sure they'll go a lot easier on you if you come forward."

"I can't."

"You have to."

Now he's crying again. And even though I know he's made these choices, he's brought this pain on himself, I can't help but feel sorry. In fact, if feels like my heart is breaking for him.

"Why don't you go upstairs," I say in a calm voice. "Just take a shower and change your clothes. Then we can talk about this some more."

He sort of nods, but I can tell he's not thinking clearly.

"Hurry. Get cleaned up, and I'll try to think of something."

"Okay."

As soon as he's gone, I go outside and call Ebony on my cell phone. And even though I'm sure Zach might kill me if he knew, I tell her everything.

"Is there any way you can help him?"

"I don't know, Samantha."

"I shouldn't have called you."

"No, you did the right thing. Let me do some investigating, and I'll get back to you. Is Zach still home?"

"He is for now. But I don't think he will be for long."

"I'll call you as soon as I know anything. But tell Zach that if he's smart, he won't try to run. If his car really has been impounded and searched, there will already be a warrant out for him. It'll only make it harder on him to run."

"I'll tell him." Then I hang up and go back into the house. I can't hear water running, so I assume he's already taken his shower. Or maybe he snuck out. Zach used to climb out his dormer window and slide down the roof onto the garage. I wouldn't be surprised if he did it today. But when I tiptoe by his room, pushing the partially closed door open, I see that Zach is still wearing his grubby clothes and sacked out on top of his bed. But at least he's still here.

I go back downstairs and wait for Ebony to call back. I feel guilty for imposing on her like this. But she didn't seem to mind. In fact, she actually seems to care. I remember, as I wait, what Mom said about how Ebony might feel guilty—about how she might be trying to make up for something. I so hope that's not the case. But even if it is, I guess I don't care. All I want is for her to help Zach. Not that I want to see him totally getting out of this. He needs to account for his stupidity, and he needs help with his addiction problem. But at the same time, I don't want to see him locked up for the next twenty years either.

The cell phone rings and I jump. But I answer it before the second ring, and to my relief it's Ebony.

"His car was towed and impounded because it was left in a dangerous place. It was partially on the road where there was a tight curve."

"And?"

"According to my sources, there wasn't anything illegal found inside it. Zach will be ticketed and fined for leaving his car there. But there isn't a warrant for his arrest."

"Really?"

"According to my sources, it's just routine."

"But what about what I told you?" I ask in a meek voice.

"Zach needs help, Samantha."

"I know."

"We could use this to get him help."

"How?"

So Ebony tells me about a rehab place she knows about where she could get him in with very little waiting.

"How's that possible? The last time he went in—it was an inpatient program for drugs. We had to wait six weeks, and then they could only keep him for thirty days. In the end, my mom thought it was just a waste of money."

"I know we could get him in because it's run by my brother."

"Where is it?"

"Washington State."

"Is it expensive?"

"I think they have a sliding scale."

"What's that?" I ask.

"It's where patients pay according to what they can afford. Do you think we could convince him to go, Samantha?"

"I think it's worth a try."

"Does your mom know about this yet?"

"Well, she has her suspicions about him getting involved in drugs again. She told me as much today."

"But she doesn't know about his car and what he just told you?"

"No."

"Do you mind if I call her?"

"Go ahead. Try her work number first."

"Okay. But before I hang up, do you want to pray for him with me, Samantha?"

"Yes!"

So we pray and then hang up. And for the first time in weeks, I feel a faint flicker of hope for my slightly lost brother. Even so I continue praying. I walk around the house and pray that God will keep Zach asleep and safe in our house until we can figure this thing out. And I pray that Ebony will say the right things to Mom and that Mom will understand and not be offended by Ebony's desire to help. And then I pray that Ebony's brother really will be able to take Zach. The sooner the better.

It's dark by the time Mom gets home. But Zach is still asleep. Just more proof that he really has been using something. He usually crashes like this after a binge with a drug like meth or speed.

"Did Ebony get ahold of you?" I ask.

"Yes." She looks worried. "Is Zach still here?"

I nod. "Crashed. Coming off something, I guess."

"Good."

"Did she tell you about Zach's car?" I ask in a low-ered voice. "About the fact that he was carrying drugs?"

Mom nods as she takes off her coat and hangs it in the coat closet. She looks so tired.

"Did she tell you about her brother's place?"

"Yes. She said that she'd already called him after talking to you, and he assured her of a spot for Zach."

"So, he's going?" I ask hopefully.

"If he agrees."

"Oh."

"Ebony offered to come by this evening. She said we can do an intervention of sorts. And she'll put some pressure on him."

"Good."

"In the meantime, we're supposed to just act normal." Mom kind of laughs. "Like I even know what that is anymore."

"You and me both."

"Why don't we start by ordering pizza? Can you take care of that?"

"Sure."

"I'm going to change clothes. The cuffs of my pants have been soggy ever since the parade."

"What if Zach gets up?"

"Tell him we ordered pizza," she says. "His favorite kind."

I nod. "Okay. He'll probably be starving."

"Yeah, he usually is." Then she trudges up the stairs, but I notice that she stops to look at the photo of our family, the one where we're happily standing together in

front of Disneyland. She lets out a tired sigh then continues on up.

I wonder what Dad would think if he could see us
today. Wouldn't it break his heart to know what Zach has
been up to during these past twenty-four hours? I can't
bear to imagine it myself. Then I wonder why God didn't
let me in on this. Why didn't He give me a vision for
Zach? Why was I busy finding Conrad's lost sister, Katie,
when my very own brother was far more lost? Doesn't
God think Zach is just as important? Then I remind myself
that help is on its way. And isn't it up to God to figure out
what's best anyway?

Fourteen

The pizza delivery van and a police car pull up in front of our house at the same time. I quickly pay the curious pizza guy as I let Ebony and a uniformed officer inside.

"Are you going to arrest him?" I whisper to Ebony.

She shakes her head. "No, it's just for effect."

"Oh." Still, I feel unsure as I direct them toward the family room, where Mom is waiting, looking as if she's sitting on a porcupine.

Zach woke up about twenty minutes ago. Mom told him to grab a shower before the pizza got here, but he's coming down the stairs now, barefoot and wearing sweats. His hair is still wet. And despite telling myself that this is a good thing, I feel so guilty. Like I'm leading the poor innocent lamb to the slaughter. I just hope I can trust Ebony. I hope she was telling me the truth.

I hold out the pizza box. "It just got here," I say in a slightly shaky voice. "Good timing, huh? Mom's in there." I nod toward the family room, worried that Zach can see right through my little act. Does he already know what's up? Is he about to bolt straight for the front door and make a run for it?

151

But instead he simply removes the pizza box from my hands, takes a big sniff, and announces he's starved as he casually strolls toward the family room. I hold my breath as I follow him. Then he stops in his tracks, so quickly that I almost stumble into him.

He looks at Mom. "What's going on?"

"Come and sit down," Mom tells him in a surprisingly calm voice.

I take the pizza box from him and go over to set it on the counter. *Breathe and just relax. Everything is going to be okay.* But when I turn around, Zach is just standing there, looking more scared than I've ever seen him before. I'm still not sure that he doesn't plan on running.

"I'm Detective Hamilton." Ebony shows him her badge. Then she extends her hand for him to shake. But he doesn't take it. "And this is Officer Reinhart," she continues, ignoring his snub.

"Why are you here?" he asks in a voice that reminds me of when he was about ten years old.

"We need to talk to you," she tells him. "We need to ask you some questions."

"Sit down, Zach," Mom tells him in a kind but firm voice.

Zach turns and looks at me now, but I just shrug, acting as if I have no idea what's coming down. Then I go over and sit down, and to my relief, Zach does the same.

"We know all about your car, Zach," Ebony begins. "It was towed and impounded, and we know about what you were carrying in it."

Zach looks at Mom now, and I can tell he's really upset. "Do you know too?"

She just nods then looks down at her hands in her lap.

"It wasn't mine," he tells her.

"Whose was it?" she asks, looking up.

"A friend—" Then he stops himself. "Not a friend. Just this guy I met. I don't even know his name."

"But you knew what it was that you were carrying in your car?" probes Ebony.

"I didn't actually see it," he says quickly. "I mean, it could've been anything."

"Did he pay you for transporting it?"

"No."

"Not yet anyway…" she suggests.

"He *didn't* pay me."

"And he probably *won't* be paying you any time soon," says Officer Reinhart in a slightly sarcastic tone.

Zach leans over and looks down at his bare feet. "No…"

"This is the deal," Ebony says in a very serious voice. "We will work with you, Zach, but only if you'll work with us."

He looks up. "What does that mean?"

"It means if you give us the guy's name and whatever you know about him, we'll figure out a way to let you off this time."

His eyes light up. "You will?"

She nods. "But only in return for your cooperation."

"You won't charge me? You can promise that?"

"As long as you cooperate and agree to our conditions."

"What are your conditions?"

So she goes into an explanation of how he must make an affidavit that will help to catch and convict the meth dealer and finally how he must agree to an inpatient drug rehab treatment.

"And that's it?" He looks skeptical. "Then you let me off?"

"Unless there's something we don't know about." She peers curiously at him, and suddenly I'm worried that there could be more. Zach could be in deeper than any of us suspect.

"How long is the rehab?" he asks.

"A minimum of sixty days. Longer if it's determined necessary."

He looks at Mom now. "But...we can't really afford it, can we? I mean, last time you said that—"

"It's all taken care of, Zach. Money isn't an issue right now."

He looks back at Ebony and frowns. "*Sixty* days?"

"Possibly longer."

"Look," says Officer Reinhart, "once your drug-dealing buddy finds out that you messed up and that you lost what you were supposed to be delivering, well, you might just want to be gone sixty days or even longer. You follow me?"

Zach slowly nods. "Yeah..."

Ebony pulls a piece of paper out of her briefcase. "This is an electronic ticket," she tells my mom. "Round-trip for the two of you to Seattle. Zach will be picked up at Sea-Tac by a counselor, and we'll put you up for the night in an airport hotel, and you can fly out early Sunday morning. Zach's return trip is open-ended."

"Who paid for this?" my mom asks.

"The precinct," says Ebony.

"Why?"

"Because Zach is a cop's kid," says Officer Reinhart. "And we stand by our brothers and their families."

Ebony looks at Zach now. "Are you ready to go?"

"Right now?"

She nods. "The Seattle flight leaves Portland International at 9:45 tonight."

"Tonight?" Zach looks like he's having second thoughts already.

"Did you want to stick around town?" asks the officer. "See if your drug-dealing buddy shows up to collect from you?"

"No," he mutters.

"Then pack your stuff." Ebony hands him a paper. "This is a list of what you can and cannot take with you. If you forget anything, your mom can send it to you later."

"Do you want help?" I follow Zach up the stairs. He doesn't answer, but I keep going anyway. No way do I want him pulling a second-story escape right now.

"This is so cool." I watch him pull a duffle sack out of his closet. "A real answer to prayer."

"Whose prayer?" he grumbles.

"Mine."

"Thanks a lot."

"Hey, would you rather go to jail?"

"Rehab is just another form of jail, Samantha." He's shoving socks and underwear into the bag, cussing under his breath.

"At least you don't get a criminal record."

"But I get to rat on a friend."

"You said he *wasn't* a friend."

He makes a growling noise.

"I'm guessing he's not a friend anymore, Zach. Officer Reinhart is probably right. This dude will probably be really ticked at you for messing him up; he'll probably be coming after you." Of course, this makes me realize something I hadn't even considered before. "Does he know where we live?"

"I don't know..." Zach turns and glares, shaking a pair of wrinkled Levi's at me. "Do ya mind, Samantha? I want to put on my jeans now. Some privacy, please?"

But somehow I know that's not what he really has in mind. Call it intuition or just an educated guess, but I'm certain that he's thinking he could still make a fast break. He could get me out of here, grab that bag and his shoes, and head right out the window.

"Why don't you just wear those sweats." I nod to the loose navy pants he's wearing. "With all the new security machines at the airports, those buttons on your Levi's would probably just set off all the alarms anyway. Olivia told me that her sister was practically strip-searched one time just because she had on—"

"Fine!" he snaps, stuffing the jeans into his bag and zipping it. "Whatever!"

Then, feeling extremely relieved and slightly victorious, I wait for him to exit his room then follow him back downstairs.

"Can we give you guys a lift to the airport?" offers Ebony.

"Do we have a choice?" grumbles Zach.

"You *do* have a choice!" my mom says to Zach in a tightly controlled yet very angry tone.

"Huh?" He looks slightly stunned by Mom's sudden show of emotion. She doesn't usually let her feelings out like this.

"No one is going to force you to do this, Zach!" The volume reaches a level that outsiders seldom hear. "You could run away right now, and maybe you wouldn't even get caught for a while. But you would get caught *eventually*! Everyone gets caught eventually." Her eyes fill with tears, and her voice cracks as she continues. "We're doing this to give you another chance, Zach. Everyone has gone to a lot of trouble to give you a second chance. Do you want to throw it away? To just spit on it and—"

"No," he says quickly. "I'm ready to go, Mom."

"Good." She turns to Ebony, straightening her shoulders. "A ride to the airport would be very much appreciated."

Mom quickly gathers some of her things and then suggests I spend the night at Olivia's again, which sounds good to me. Then blinking back tears, I tell Zach good-bye and that I'll be praying for him. He just rolls his eyes at me, and throws the strap of his bag over his shoulder then walks out the door, dragging his heels like someone who's been condemned to the electric chair.

I'm so glad he doesn't know that I'm the one who called Ebony today. He so could've gotten away with this whole thing, and if he had any idea that I'm the one who ratted on him…well, I just don't want to consider that right now.

Mostly, I believe that God intervened on Zach's behalf tonight. And I'm thankful.

Suddenly everyone is gone, and I realize how quiet the house is. And it's just me. Me and the uneaten pizza. I take out a lukewarm slice and then, feeling slightly spooked, call Olivia. Between bites and after swearing her to absolute secrecy, I pour out the story of Zach.

"Man, you have had one freaky busy day, Samantha."

"Tell me about it. And I hate to impose on your hospitality again, but I'm kinda scared about being alone here tonight. Especially if Zach's drug friend is anywhere around or if he's feeling particularly vengeful, you know? Do you think I could—?"

"I'm on my way," she says. "Be there in a few."

"Thanks."

Olivia and I don't stay up nearly as late tonight as we did last night. I can barely keep my eyes open when my head hits the pillow. But it's good to feel safe, and before I fall asleep I pray for Zach. And then for Mom. Then I thank God for intervening for us tonight. And then I drift off into blissful sleep.

———

I wake up suddenly, my heart is racing, and every muscle in my body is tensed up—like I'm ready to run for my life. I don't know where I am or why I feel this need to escape, but after a few seconds, and thanks to the light coming from her bathroom, I realize that I'm in Olivia's bedroom, sleeping in the bed across from hers. The house is calm and quiet. There's no real reason to be afraid. It was only a bad dream.

I try to relax and to recall what the dream was, and after a bit, I realize that it's almost the exact same dream I had before. The one where my hands and feet were tied and duct tape covered my mouth. Once again the small, dark room was hot and dry, and I was extremely thirsty. Then the door opened, and I saw the menacing silhouette of a man coming in, and I knew that he was going to hurt me badly, or maybe even kill me.

But the last thing I remember about the dream was that I was not the one who was tied up and helpless. Suddenly I found myself standing a few feet away, in a dark corner of the room, just watching and wondering what I could do to help this person who was bound and gagged and lying on the mattress on the floor.

But here's the weird part, I just assumed that the girl tied up had to be Kayla. But with the light coming through the slightly opened door, I could see the girl's face, and it wasn't Kayla at all. This girl had dark hair and dark eyes and seemed to be Hispanic. And not unlike Kayla, she was very pretty. But the thing I remember most was the look of pure terror in those big dark eyes, almost as if she was looking at the devil. Chills run down my spine just to remember this. And I must pray and pray and pray before I'm finally able to go to sleep again.

I tell Olivia about my dream first thing in the morning. "Do you think I got it wrong?" I finally ask.

"Wrong?" She sets a cup of coffee in front of me.

"In thinking that Kayla was being held against her will?"

"I don't know..."

"I mean, the other time, you know, when I had that similar dream, I just sort of assumed it was about Kayla, but I never actually saw her. In that dream, I was the one who was tied up...and it was so horrible. I felt so totally miserable and helpless and scared. But I assumed it was God's way of showing me that Kayla was in serious trouble. And now I see that it wasn't Kayla at all. What if I'm all wrong about everything? What if I'm just having weird nightmares that don't mean anything?"

"Do you think it was just a nightmare, Samantha?"

"No...not really. It seemed to be more than that."

"Maybe God is trying to show you that someone else needs help," Olivia says as she opens a box of cereal. "I mean, even if you don't know this girl, you'd still want to help her, wouldn't you?"

"Yeah, of course. But I feel like I've led Ebony down the wrong path now. Making her believe that Kayla's the one in trouble down in Arizona. It's like I've gotten my signals all mixed up or something."

Olivia laughs. "So it *is* like receiving signals?"

I smile and take the box of cereal from her. "It's kind of hard to describe."

"Good morning, girls," says Mrs. Marsh. "You're sure up bright and early. Going to church today?"

"Yeah," says Olivia. "Want to come?"

Mrs. Marsh actually seems to consider this. "Not today, Livvie. But do let me know when the special

Christmas service is, and maybe Dad and I will come then." She winks at me. "Yeah, I know what you're thinking, Samantha. We've turned into those twice-a-year kinds of churchgoers. Christmas and Easter."

"I didn't say that."

"I know you didn't. But Olivia says it often enough."

"Well, it's kind of true," says Olivia. "You used to go all the time when we were little kids. You'd drag us there whether we wanted to go or not."

Her mom smiles. "We thought it was the right thing to do. Now you kids are old enough to take yourselves to church. And sometimes your dad and I are just plain tired. We like to relax on Sundays. Does that make us bad people?"

"As long as you love the Lord and you're still praying and reading your Bible, well, I'm not going to worry about it too much," Olivia tells her mom.

"Well, we do and we are. And maybe someday when work and life lighten up, we'll get back into the churchgoing habit too."

While I understand Olivia's desire for her parents to attend church more regularly, I'm thinking that at least they're still living like Christians. I can't actually say that much for my mom. More and more, I don't really know where she stands with God. And I have to admit that it worries me. But instead of worrying about it, which I've been trying to do less of lately, I take a few moments to pray for her while I get dressed for church.

First I pray that God gives her a safe flight back home and that she's not too worn out from all this Zach stuff.

And then I pray that somehow God will manage to get her attention and to remind her that she needs Him. Maybe now more than ever.

Fifteen

I call Ebony during lunch on Monday. First I thank her for helping with Zach this weekend. And then I tell her about my most recent dream and how I'm worried that I might have led her down the wrong path by assuming the previous nightmare was about Kayla.

"Because," I finally admit, "as it turns out, it wasn't Kayla being held against her will…it was totally someone else. I guess I just assumed it was Kayla the other time, probably because I'd been thinking about her so much and praying for her. But this girl was definitely not Kayla." Then I briefly describe the girl in the dream to her.

"Do you think it could've been Kayla, but that someone had dyed her hair to disguise her? That happens sometimes."

"No, this girl definitely looked very Hispanic."

"Do you think you could identify her?"

"Maybe."

"Can you come by here after school?" she asks. "We could go through the missing persons photos."

"Sure," I say halfheartedly. "I'll see if Olivia can give me a ride."

I feel this cloud of discouragement hanging over me after that phone call. It's not that I don't want to help

163

someone else. I definitely do. But what if the dream doesn't mean anything? What if I'm just wasting everyone's time? And what about Kayla? What if she's still in need and I'm just not getting it? Consequently, I find myself praying for Kayla off and on throughout the afternoon.

"You sure are quiet," Olivia observes as she drives me downtown.

"Sorry."

"Still feeling badly about Kayla?"

"Yeah. I just wish we could find her. It's almost winter break, and then Christmas. It just seems like she should be coming home by now."

"All you can do is what God puts before you, Samantha."

"I know..."

Then we're at the precinct, and I thank her and tell her that I'll catch a ride home with my mom afterward. "I know you need to practice for the Christmas concert. Thanks for taking the time to do this."

"No problem."

I feel more nervous than before as I walk toward Ebony's office. It's like my confidence is shaken. And I feel that, even more than usual, I have absolutely no control over this "gift" that I've been given. Is it even real? Maybe I'm just imagining everything. Maybe my mom is right—I'm getting in over my head and I'll be needing serious psychological help before long.

Help me, God, I pray silently and helplessly as I stand outside Ebony's door. *If this is of You, please, help me to handle it right. Help me to stay tuned in to You; help me to help others for Your sake. Amen.*

"Hey, Samantha." Ebony comes down the hallway toward me carrying a couple of sodas, one that she hands to me. "How's it going?"

I kind of shrug. "I don't know..."

"Feeling bad about Zach?" She opens her office door, and we both go inside.

"No." I sit down. "It's actually kind of a relief knowing that he's off getting help right now. I don't have to worry that we're going to get a late night phone call from the police informing us that he's done something wrong or is hurt or even, well, you know."

"I know. My brother, the one who runs the rehab place in Washington, had some problems himself as a kid. But he got help and decided he wanted to help others. Zach is in good hands."

"Yeah, I figured he was."

"So, what're you feeling so bummed about?"

"Kayla."

"Oh..." She nods.

"I just thought we were on this trail, you know, and that she was going to turn up like...like yesterday."

"Unfortunately, it's not usually that easy."

"But then having the same dream about this total stranger, well, I guess I'm sort of doubting myself."

"What about God? Are you doubting Him too?"

"No," I say quickly. "Of course not."

Ebony smiles. "Then just relax, Samantha. Let God handle this. Remember, you're just the vessel."

"Just the vessel…"

"Yes. If God wants to pour some information into you, He will. If not, well, there's nothing you can do about it. Right?"

I smile. "You mean I can't control God?"

She laughs. "Nope. But don't we wish we could sometimes?" Then she motions for to me to come around to the other side of her desk. "I have some photos for you to look at on my computer. I asked Eric to do some sifting for me. Just missing Hispanic girls between the ages of twelve and twenty-five. Have a seat and start scanning through them. If you find any that seem familiar, make a note of their names. Okay?"

"Okay."

"I've got to go take care of something else right now. You mind being here on your own?"

"That's fine."

So I sit here and go through the photos, but the more photos I look at, the more confused I begin to feel. It's like they're all starting to look exactly the same, and while some of them do seem to resemble the girl I saw in my dream, I couldn't say so for certain.

Finally, I lean back in the chair and just close my eyes and try to relax. It's like there's this big knot between my shoulder blades, and I know that I'm starting to stress out over this. And why shouldn't I? I mean, this is crazy. How am I, a mere sixteen-year-old girl—okay, seventeen next month—supposed to solve crimes about people I don't even know, committed in states where I've never even been before? How is that even possible?

All things are possible with God.

Now, although I didn't hear those words audibly, I did hear them in my heart. Furthermore, I know that those words are true. I just need to trust Him more. I say another prayer and take a deep breath, trying to just relax.

I open my eyes and scan down through a few more photos of smiling dark-haired, dark-eyed Hispanic girls, and just as I'm starting to feel like this is totally hopeless, I come to the next photo, and I nearly fall out of Ebony's chair. I stare hard, wondering if I'm just imagining this or if it's for real. Then to test myself, I go back and look through some of the other photos until I'm back at this one again. But I know that this is her. There's something in her eyes or the shape of her face or maybe it's her nose, but something about this photo seems right. Suddenly I feel positive. This is the girl!

I write down the girl's name, big and bold, and even put an exclamation mark at the end of it before I set off to find Ebony. Instead I find Officer Reinhart, and Eric tells me that Ebony is still busy.

"Any luck with the photos?" he asks.

"Yes! I was about to give up, and then I saw this one." I hand him the slip of paper with the girl's name.

"Elena Maiesa," he says. "Sounds Hispanic anyway."

"Yes. She is."

"I'll see what I can find out about her."

"Good." I stand there expectantly, thinking he'll probably want to get to work on it right now.

He laughs. "I probably won't get to it today, Samantha."

"Oh." I nod. "Yeah, of course not. Well, I better go."

"We'll let you know what we find out, okay?"

"Thanks."

It's just a little past four as I leave the precinct, which means I'll be spending the next couple of hours waiting for mom to get off work. As I walk up to the park district building, I hear shouts and laughter coming from the day care playground, where kids are probably enjoying their afternoon recess. And this gives me an idea. First I stop by administration and give Mom's assistant a message; then I head back downstairs to the day care center.

"Hey, Samantha," says Kellie. "What's up?"

"I wondered if you could use some help this afternoon. I have a couple of hours to kill and—"

"Man, did you come to the right place!" She grins. "We're just starting to work on Christmas presents this week." She holds up a plastic bag filled with white powder. "Handprints set in plaster of Paris. Kind of messy. Some extra help would be fantastic."

So the next thing I know, I'm wearing a bright-colored apron and helping kids to plant their paws into the plaster goop forms that Rachel, another teacher, has all ready for them in the eating area. Then, keeping their hands off the walls and chairs and other children, I usher them back to the bathroom to wash up before their fingers get hard and stiff. After that I escort them back to their classroom where Kellie is just starting story time. It's like a three-ring circus.

"I'm so glad you stopped in," Kellie says when we're finally done and the kids are starting to get picked up by their parents. "It would've been crazy without you."

"Hey, it was fun. And it helped to pass the time."

"How about coming back to work here during Christmas break again this year?" she suggests. "You were great last year."

"I didn't know you needed help."

"Well, Rachel just announced that she wants time off to go back east to see her family, which means we'll be seriously shorthanded for a couple weeks. I'd figured on hiring subs to fill in, but we'd much rather have you. You know how the kids love you."

"Sure," I tell her. "That sounds great, and I could use the extra money."

"Couldn't we all."

So as we're discussing details and schedule, my mom pops her head into the day care center. "I'm here to pick up my little girl."

"Hi, Mommy!" I say back in a childish voice, which makes a couple of the straggler kids laugh. "I'm ready to go home now."

I feel hopeful that Mom might be happier now, knowing that Zach is in treatment and life is calming down some. But as we drive home, I can tell that she's still pretty uptight. My first clue is when she starts griping about the traffic and some of the drivers' less-than-stellar driving skills, and eventually, as we get closer to home, she's complaining about the weather, which has turned windy and cold. And finally she's just grumbling about Christmas and work and basically everything about life in general.

"Something wrong?" I finally ask, knowing I could be sorry for this inquiry later.

"Do I sound that bad?"

"Sort of." I sigh. "I thought maybe you'd be feeling good today. I mean, knowing that Zach's okay."

"Yes. I should be thankful, shouldn't I?" Still I can hear the bitter edge to her voice, and I don't respond.

"It's not that I'm not glad about Zach getting some help, Samantha. Really, I am. It's just that this is *not* how I imagined my life would go. You know, at this stage of the game, well, I didn't see myself working so hard at my job, or that my husband would get shot and I'd be a single mom struggling to make ends meet. Or having a kid who's a junkie and gets picked up by the police to go into rehab. It's just not the life I'd planned for myself."

"I guess no one really knows how things will turn out…"

She glances at me. "Well, besides you anyway."

"I don't know much of anything. I mean, unless God shows me. And He never showed me anything regarding Zach."

We're home now, and Mom just lets out a long exasperated sigh. "I'm sorry. I shouldn't vent on you like that. It's just that I don't have anyone else to let my hair down with."

"It's okay."

"No, it's not. Maybe I'm just tired. What with Zach and Saturday's late night trip to Seattle, this was a long weekend." She dumps her coat and bag onto the bench by the door.

"Why don't you just relax? Take a hot bath or something. I can make us something for dinner."

"Oh, that sounds great, Samantha." She gives me a small smile. "I appreciate it. Sorry about my little pity party."

"It's okay. I understand."

In fact, I may understand even better than I realized. Because now, as I go into the kitchen and try to find something that can be transformed into something that will resemble a meal, I start feeling kind of like Mom just described. Kind of like, this isn't very fair. I mean, this isn't exactly the sort of life I had wanted either. I don't enjoy having a grumpy, full-time working mom. And it's not easy losing your dad when you're only twelve. And pile up Zach's drug problems on top of everything else, and suddenly I feel the need to have a little pity party all of my own.

Instead I dig in the freezer until I find a packaged lasagna dinner that looks slightly frostbitten. But I figure it's worth a try, and maybe I can put some extra cheese on top. Then as the oven is preheating, I pull out my Bible and open it up to a familiar passage.

> "Are you tired? Worn out? Burned out on religion? Come to me. Get away with me and you'll recover your life. I'll show you how to take a real rest. Walk with me and work with me—watch how I do it. Learn the unforced rhythms of grace. I won't lay anything heavy or ill-fitting on you. Keep company with me and you'll learn to live freely and lightly."
> (Matthew 11:28–30)

As I set the table for Mom and me, I run these thoughts through my head. I ponder what it means to live freely and lightly as I get some frozen peas ready to be nuked in the microwave. Finally I decide that this is a Bible verse I should memorize, so I write it down on one of the index cards that I keep especially for this sort of thing. Then I set it on the table by my plate. Maybe I should even share it with my mom before we eat our dinner. I think she's in need of it as much as I am.

The next few days pass rather uneventfully. I try not to worry about the girl in my dream; instead, I find myself praying for her. Her name, Elena Maiesa, seems to be engraved into my memory, along with her face. But so far I've heard nothing from Ebony about her. In fact, I've heard nothing from Ebony at all. I've been tempted to call her, but I figure she'd have called me if anything new had happened. More likely she's involved in something else. Maybe something more important.

I continue to pray for Kayla too. But more and more I'm thinking that maybe I was all wrong. Maybe Kayla is perfectly fine. Maybe she's already married to her Colby friend and living happily ever after. Yeah, right.

I go to Olivia's winter concert with her and am pleased when Conrad comes and sits beside me. I'd started to give up on him too, but it seems like he's still interested in me. Afterward, he invites Olivia and me to meet him and Alex for coffee. And without even checking with Olivia, I accept for us. But when I meet her backstage, she seems happy about the news.

"Really?" she says with bright eyes. "Alex too?"

"Yeah. Great concert by the way. Your solo was awesome."

"Thanks." She looks down at her black concert dress. "Man, I wish I'd brought something to change into. I didn't know we'd be going out for coffee afterward."

"Hey, you look beautiful. Glamorous. Like a star."

She grins. "Lay it on, Samantha."

"Seriously, you really do."

"Well, let me get my coat."

And then we drive over to Lava Java, where the guys are already waiting for us. Okay, it's not a date, but it feels like the beginning of something.

"Good job tonight," Conrad says after we've ordered coffees and joined them. "You did a fantastic job on that solo."

"Yeah," adds Alex. "That was the best song of the whole night."

Olivia is beaming now, but she simply says a calm "thanks," and then changes the subject. "Mr. Lowry said this might be the last year to do songs like 'O Holy Night.' Some lady on the school board is talking about banning all songs of religious nature from the curriculum."

"Right," says Alex. "So you can just sing songs like 'Jingle Bells' and 'Frosty the Snowman.' That'd be pretty sophisticated."

"Or 'The Twelve Days of Christmas,'" adds Conrad. "There's a song with substance."

"Hey, I like 'The Twelve Days,'" I protest. "We used to sing it with my dad on our way to get a Christmas tree when we were kids. It was our tradition."

"Speaking of that song," says Conrad. "Alex's family had the weirdest thing happen last Christmas. Tell the girls what happened."

Then Alex proceeds to tell us how his family got these strange anonymous thank-you cards for gifts his family had never sent. "The first one was just kind of odd. It said something like: 'Thank you so much for your thoughtful gift of a partridge; he is a very lovely bird. However, we're not quite sure what to do with the pear tree since it is winter and too early to plant right now.'"

We all laugh.

"But then it just kept going. We got a new thank-you each day. And of course, they loved the five golden rings and said something like, 'Oh, you shouldn't have...' but then the thank-yous started getting a little irate. Like they'd say, 'Thanks a lot for those seven geese and all those eggs, but enough already. They're making a mess of our backyard and harassing the six swans, and the neighbors are complaining about the noise from those four calling birds. Please, stop this nonsense immediately, or we shall contact the authorities!'"

By the time Alex reaches the end of his dramatically told story, we're all laughing so hysterically that Olivia and I have tears running down our cheeks.

"No way," Olivia says as she wipes her eyes. "They really sent those to you?"

He nods. "My mom saved them. It was really weird."

"Did you ever figure out who did it?" asks Conrad.

"My dad insists it's this crazy dude at work, but the guy denies it." He laughs. "It's a mystery."

"What a great joke," says Olivia.

Finally, it's time to go, but as we leave, Conrad and Alex both suggest that we get together again. "Maybe during winter break," says Alex.

"Cool," I tell him.

"You guys ever go ice-skating?" asks Olivia, who used to take lessons.

"We used to play hockey," Alex says with a slightly cocky grin.

"But it's been quite a while," admits Conrad.

"I haven't skated in years," I say. "But it used to be fun."

"Let's do it," says Conrad. Then he winks at me. "I'll give you a call, Samantha."

We wave good-bye and head off to our cars. "That was so cool," Olivia says as she unlocks her car.

"Yeah," I admit. "The most fun I've had in ages."

"And it wasn't really a date."

"Nope, it wasn't."

And as she drives us home, I'm thinking I could use a few more fun times like this in my life. It seems the past few weeks have been heavy and hard. And I appreciate the fact that God wants to give us some breaks. He wants us to laugh and play and have a good time, and hey, I could get used to this.

Sixteen

Winter break officially began last Friday, and now I'm working at the park district day care center. Okay, it's not exactly a glamorous job, but it's kind of fun, and the kids do like me, and it helps to pass the time. Plus, I'll get paid.

The first several days of "vacation" pass fairly uneventfully. Just work and life and nothing out of the ordinary. No more dreams or visions or much of anything unusual. And I still haven't heard a word from Ebony about either of the missing girls, nothing about Elena or Kayla, but I continue to pray for them daily, if not more.

However, I'm starting to think that my dreams and visions may have been nothing more than my overactive imagination. And in a way, I suppose this is a relief. I have no problem living like a regular high school girl.

In fact, last night, Olivia and I actually met Conrad and Alex for a prearranged ice-skating debut. I hadn't skated since before Dad died, but with Conrad's patient help and coaching, it slowly came back to me. Meanwhile, Olivia and Alex really cut up the ice like a couple of pros. By the time the evening was over and we reconvened at Lava Java for something to warm up with, we were all exhausted but thoroughly happy. I never mentioned the blisters on my heels. It was worth it. And Conrad hinted that we should all go see a movie together this Saturday. No complaints from me there either.

But then as Mom and I are driving to work this morning, and I'm feeling only half-awake and just blurrily looking out the window, I see this billboard with a travel ad promoting the Southwest. Mom's stopped at the red light, and I just blankly stare at the billboard.

Then instead of seeing the red-golden mountains, a big cactus in the foreground, and the bright aqua-blue sky behind it, I see a girl lying on her side in the dirt. Just like in my previous dream, her mouth is taped with duct tape, but her face is bruised and so swollen that I can't tell who she is. As before, her hands and feet are bound. But her long hair is matted with dirt and dust, so much that I can't tell what color it is, just a dull sandy brown color. But the skin on her bare arms and legs looks pale, as if the blood is drained out. Somehow I know that this girl is dead. I gasp loudly just as Mom pulls into the intersection.

"What?" She starts to brake and looks both ways. "Is a car coming?"

"No, it's okay."

"What then?" she asks in an irritated voice as she carefully proceeds through the intersection. "Why did you do that? You scared me, Samantha."

"Sorry," I say quickly. "I just thought of something and, well, sorry."

"Well, don't do that! Especially when I'm driving. I thought we were about to get hit."

I consider telling her about what I just saw, but then it will only disturb her. She won't understand. And she might even get mad. Instead I just ponder on what flashed so quickly before me, trying to remember the details. But mostly I know that she's dead. This girl has been killed. I could be wrong, but I strongly suspect that this girl is either Elena or Kayla, and it makes me feel sick inside. As Mom pulls into the parking lot, my throat feels like someone wedged a stone in there, and hot tears are building in my eyes.

"I have to make a phone call," I tell Mom as I get out of the car, pulling out my cell phone and turning away so she won't see my face.

"Catch you later," she calls out, and I hear her heels clicking across the pavement toward the building.

I hit the speed dial for Ebony's number, expecting to get her voice mail, but instead she picks up. I quickly relay my vision to her, finally saying, "Someone is dead, Ebony. And it's either Elena or Kayla. I can't explain how, but I just know it."

"Oh…" Her voice sounds sad.

"The girl I saw had to have been murdered."

"It's just been so busy around here lately, Samantha. I know that Eric was doing some searching for Elena, but I don't think he came up with anything yet. And we haven't learned anything new about Kayla. Oh, I'm so sorry to hear this. Are you certain the girl was really dead? How can you know this for sure?"

I consider this. "Well, I *felt* like she was dead. I mean, she looked dead. It seemed very real."

"But you told me that some of your visions are about things that haven't happened yet. Do you think that might possibly be the case with this?"

"I, uh, I don't know. It's not like God puts a time and date on these things." I kind of laugh, but I can still feel the tears chilling in the breeze on my face.

"I know...but it's possible, isn't it? Do you think this girl, whoever she is, might still be alive?"

Suddenly I feel hopeful. "Maybe that's it. Maybe God was showing me what would happen if this girl isn't rescued, Ebony. But is there any real chance that she will be rescued in time?"

"I have no idea, but we've been in close contact with the FBI about all of this, and I'll let them know that they need to really get moving on it. Not that they'll take me seriously." She sighs. "As you can imagine, it's been a little hard to explain to them where we've been getting our leads."

I glance at my watch and realize that I need to get to work now. "Let me know if I can be of any more help. Okay?"

"I will. You're working at the day care center today?"

"Yeah."

"Keep your phone on, will you?"

"Yeah, no problem."

"I'll let you know if we learn anything."

I feel a tiny bit of relief knowing that Ebony is on this, but at the same time I feel extremely sad, and the vision of the dead girl feels like it's been imprinted into my memory.

"You okay?" Kellie asks as I punch my time card.

"Yeah." I force a smile for her benefit.

"You don't look okay." She peers at me more closely. "Sure you're not coming down with something? That flu's been going around. Already I've had calls from about ten parents saying that their kids are sick."

"That's too bad." I hang up my coat. "But I'm sure I'm okay." Then I head over to where Spencer looks like he's about ready to punch Damon and quickly break it up. Somehow, Spencer has gotten the idea that Damon is his mortal enemy and consequently requires a lot of extra attention.

"Good catch," Kellie calls out as I lead Spencer over to the time-out bench for a quick little talk.

Just as we sit down, the phone that I've placed in my pocket is starting to ring.

"You better answer that," Spencer says in a smart-aleck voice.

"Yeah, and you better just sit here and wait until I'm done."

He scowls.

"Hello?" I say into the phone.

"This is Ebony, Samantha. I know you're at work, but I just thought of something. When you had that vision this morning, did you notice any of the surrounding area? Any landscape features, buildings, or anything?"

"I'm not sure," I say as I hold on to squirming Spencer's arm. I'm pretty sure if I let go, he'll take off and probably really clobber poor Damon. "Maybe. I guess I didn't really think about it much at the time. I mean, I was mostly looking at the, uh, the girl."

"Is there any chance you could come over here this afternoon? I thought maybe I could get Michael Taylor back in, and maybe you guys could work on a drawing."

I glance over to where Kellie is standing by the sign-in book. "I'm not sure. I could ask. Can I call you back in a few minutes?"

"Yes. I'd appreciate that."

So I deal with Spencer, and he tells me that Damon hit him first. So I tell Spencer to remain in time-out while I go off to find Damon, who does confess to hitting him first. So I release Spencer from time-out and put Damon in his place. But first I give Damon a little lecture about why we don't hit people. When all seems to be under control, I go over and speak to Kellie.

"Any chance I could get some time off this afternoon?" I ask.

"So, you really aren't feeling well?"

"Well, something's come up..."

She puts her hand on my arm. "It's okay, Samantha. Since we have fewer kids today, I don't have a problem with you taking the whole afternoon off. Just don't get sick, okay? It'd be miserable to be sick on Christmas."

"Thanks."

The morning passes very slowly, but finally lunch is served and cleaned up, and the kids are down for naps. I tell Kellie good-bye, clock out for the day, then head over to the police station.

I've already told Ebony to expect me after one, and when I get there, Michael is all ready to go.

"Hello, love," he says to me in his cheerful voice. "I hear we've got more work to do."

I attempt a smile. "I hope it's not too gruesome."

"Don't you worry, sweetie, I've probably seen and heard it all by now." He nods to a chair across from where his sketch pad is waiting. "I just want you to do like you did before. Sit down and relax and just empty out all those pesky distracting thoughts. Breathe deeply." Then he takes me through some relaxation techniques, and I lean back in the chair and try to let the stresses of the morning just slide away.

He slowly walks me back through my vision, once again asking many different questions—some that really do stir up the memory and others that seem slightly irrelevant. But used to his techniques, I cooperate. I can hear the scritch-scratch sound of his pastels as he speaks, rhythmically moving across the paper in a soothing sound that almost makes me sleepy. But I continue to answer his questions, and he continues to draw.

When we're done, I am, once again, totally amazed. *"How do you do that?"* I study the pastel drawing that is eerily similar to the vision I had earlier.

He laughs. "One could ask the same question of you, dear."

Then we make some tweaks and changes, and finally I have to admit that it looks very much like what I saw.

"How's it going in here?" Ebony sticks her head in the door. "Any progress?"

"Come and see," says Michael.

Ebony comes and looks over his shoulder then glances at me. "That's it? What you saw in your vision?"

I nod. "I'm as amazed as anyone."

She smiles. "Well, this might actually be helpful. Can I take it now, Michael? Are you all done?"

He looks at me. "All done?"

I carefully study the drawing, then remember something. "There was a shoe," I say suddenly.

"But you said her feet were bare."

"Lying on the ground," I tell him. Then I close my eyes and take a deep breath and try to remember. "It was all dirty, but it was white with three pale blue stripes."

"Like Adidas?"

"Yes," I say. "It *was* Adidas. A low-top, like one of those new lightweight running shoes. It was off to the left side of her, just lying in the dirt." I open my eyes, and already Michael is adding a shoe to the drawing.

"That's good," says Ebony. "That will be helpful."

"I don't remember Kayla wearing shoes like that," I say. "But I suppose it's possible."

"Her mother should know," says Ebony.

Then Michael proudly hands over his masterpiece.

"Off to get photographed," she tells us. "Then we'll run it over to the FBI. See if it rings any bells."

"Do you need me for anything else?" I ask.

"Well, I was thinking that, if you're not busy, could you go over to Kayla's house with me again? I was remembering how you got that vision in her bathroom. And it occurred to me that there might be other rooms that we didn't go into where you might pick up on something else, Samantha."

"Our little medium," says Michael with a chuckle.

Now I like Michael, but this comment seriously irritates me. "I am *not* a medium!"

"Oh?" He looks surprised and slightly offended.

I sigh. "Okay, I guess I am a medium—as in medium height, medium weight, and I do wear medium-sized shirts."

This makes him laugh.

"But I'm not a medium," I tell him in a kinder tone. "I'm a Christian, and I believe that God gives me these visions and dreams. But it's very different than being a medium. The Bible makes it clear that we should avoid mediums and psychics and sorcerers...and I do."

"But you *do* see dead people?" he teases, using that familiar line from that movie *The Sixth Sense*.

"This was the first time," I admit. "But I hope you can understand that it still doesn't make me a medium. And I'd appreciate it if you didn't call me that, okay?"

He nods. "Yes, I suppose you're right. Thank you for setting me straight."

"So, how about it?" says Ebony. "Want to go over to Kayla's house with me again?"

"Guess it can't hurt," I tell her. Then we tell Michael good-bye and thanks, and I go with Ebony to hand over the drawing to Eric.

"Scan it and run it," she tells him.

He studies it. "Wow, you really saw this, Samantha?"

I nod without looking at the drawing. "Pretty weird, huh?"

"Hopefully it will help us nail this creep," says Ebony. "You had lunch yet, Samantha?"

"Well, other than a couple of snitched carrot sticks, no."

So we head over to Rosie's, and I order my regular— pastrami and Swiss on rye. Then we sit down.

"Have you heard from Zach?"

"Mom got an e-mail from him on Tuesday. She said he sounded okay."

"He gets to use e-mail?"

"Only for good behavior," I tell her. "And it has to be supervised."

"That's wise."

After we're done eating, Ebony drives us to Kayla's house. But we're both quiet during the drive, and I use this time to really pray for Kayla. I ask God to protect her. I so don't want her to turn out to be the girl in the drawing. I also pray for Elena. Although I've never met this girl, it's beginning to feel as if I know her too. I don't want the girl in the drawing to be either of these girls. I don't want her to be anyone. *God, please, stop this horrible thing. Whatever it is, whoever is behind it, please, stop it, stop them. Now.*

"Kayla's mom is at work," Ebony says as she pulls into the driveway. "But she told me to feel free to go and look around. She sounds really desperate now. I think she suspects that something really is wrong. She told me that she felt certain she would've heard from Kayla by now. Or that Kayla would've contacted the aunt down in San Diego. But no one has heard anything. Mrs. Henderson is really worried."

"And it's got to be hard at Christmastime," I say as we walk up the front walk. I glance down the street to see the other houses in this family friendly neighborhood, all bearing some signs of the holidays, whether it's lights or wreaths or trees in the windows or Santa on the front lawn, but Kayla's house is conspicuously void of any decorations.

"Her mom sounds pretty depressed." Ebony gets the hidden key and unlocks the front door. "Do you want me to come in too? Or will I just be in the way?"

I consider this. "It might be better if I'm alone. I mean, that way I won't be distracted."

She nods. "That makes sense." She looks up at the sky. "But it's looking like rain. Maybe I'll wait in the car."

"Okay." Then I go into the quiet, dim house. The drapes are closed and the house has a dead, shutdown feeling to it. As if the life has all been drained out. Once again, I think about my vision and Michael's drawing, and I hope that it's not Kayla. I pray that it's not.

I slowly walk through the living room and into the kitchen. Without turning on any lights or touching anything, I just slowly move through the house. I have no idea what I'm looking for or whether or not this will work. I remember that the last time it worked it caught me completely by surprise. So I decide to pretend that I'm not actually looking for clues or hoping to get a vision. Instead, I imagine I am Kayla, just home from school and doing my normal thing.

I go and stand in front of the fridge and even open it, looking around inside to see that it's even more empty and bare than our own fridge at home. And although there's a plastic carton of something that seems to be growing green fuzz, nothing seems to really stand out. I close the refrigerator and then proceed into the family room, where I flop down on the couch that's situated across from the TV. I even reach for the remote and pretend to turn it on. Then I just sit there and blankly stare at the dark, gray screen. Nothing.

Nothing, nothing, nothing.

Finally, I'm ready to give up. After all, this is God's thing and His timing, and He's the one calling the shots. There's no way I can force Him to show me something He doesn't want revealed. Even if I wish I could.

Just before leaving, I open the hall closet. I have no idea why, but I open it and just stand there, as if I'm going to pull out a coat and head out the door. I see a pink parka with fake white fur trim around the hood. I remember seeing Kayla wearing that last year. Out of earshot, Olivia had told me that Kayla probably thought she looked like Paris Hilton in it, and we both laughed. Now I feel badly about that. I reach out and touch the sleeve of the jacket and sigh. "I'm sorry, Kayla." Then I start to close the door but am hit with a flash of light, and I stop.

I see Kayla's face now. Clearly and with no duct tape covering her mouth. "I'm sorry," she is saying with tears running down her cheeks. "I'm sorry. I'm sorry. I'm sorry." And then she is gone. That's all. I wait, hoping for something more. Something that will mean something and help us to find her. But all I see are coats and scarves and hats. Nothing out of the ordinary.

My hands are shaking as I close the closet door. I pause and consider walking through the house again, but it's already after three o'clock. I've been here for nearly an hour, and Ebony is probably getting cold out in her car. Finally, I decide to give up. But as I lock the door and walk back out to the car, it occurs to me that I should be feeling a little bit encouraged. At least Kayla was alive in this vision. That means she's not the girl lying in the dirt. At least not yet.

I tell Ebony about my vision, and she asks some questions. "Was there anything in the background?"

"No."

"Did you see what she was wearing?"

"No."

"Anything different about her hair?"

"No." I sigh. "Sorry. It's not much help, is it?"

"What about jewelry or makeup?"

I consider this. "I don't remember any earrings or anything. And no makeup either. And I guess that's kind of different since Kayla was always into jewelry and makeup."

"Yes, that's what her mother told me too."

"But I do feel hopeful," I tell her. "I mean, that she's alive. That's something, isn't it?"

She nods as she backs out of the driveway. "Yes. That is something. What do you think she was sorry about?"

"I'm not sure... At first I thought it was probably that she'd left home and stuff, like she was regretting making a stupid choice like that. But then her face seemed sort of terrified too, like she was apologizing to someone with more power than she had, like she was telling someone that she was sorry so he wouldn't hurt her. You know?"

"Yes. That had occurred to me too."

She drives in silence again and I begin to pray. I continue to beg God to protect Kayla, and Elena too. I'm certain that they're both in danger. "Do you think that Kayla and Elena could be connected?" I ask suddenly. "Like could they be in the same place together? In the same kind of trouble?"

"I've wondered about that too."

"Don't you think that if God keeps giving me visions, wouldn't that mean He plans to help them? That He'll show us where they are before it's too late?"

"It would seem that way, Samantha."

And that's what I think too. Why would God waste His time showing me these things if He didn't have a plan? I just pray that I can stay tuned in and open to hearing Him, if and when He's ready to show us something more. And I pray that I can remain patient too. Because the truth is, right now I want to shout at God. I want to shake my fist and demand to know why He doesn't just make Himself clear. Why doesn't He just speak plainly? Why is He so mysterious? And why is this taking so darn long?

Seventeen

By the end of the week and with no news about Kayla or Elena, I'm trying not to obsess over these two missing girls. I've been praying for them more than ever and hoping that somehow they might both be found before Christmas. But it's only four days away now, and I'm thinking it's probably unlikely. Still, I'm trying not to be depressed. I'm trying to trust God.

Fortunately, I can distract myself from this today. It's Saturday, and Olivia and I are going to the see the new Narnia movie with Conrad and Alex tonight! And while we're not calling it a date per se, I know that both Olivia and I are pretty jazzed about it. And Olivia decided that we should "dress up." Oh, not like we're going to a formal dance or anything as lame as that, just something a little nicer than jeans. But now as I search through my closet, trying to find that special something, I'm thinking that my old jeans are looking pretty good. Why did I agree to this?

I'm just getting ready to call Olivia to beg for some quick fashion suggestions when my cell phone rings. I quickly answer it, thinking it's probably Olivia asking me what I'm wearing, but instead it's Ebony.

"Sorry to bother you on your day off," she says.

I laugh. "That's okay. I don't really think of it like that."

"Well, there's been a new development." Her voice sounds serious, and I get a chilly feeling on my skin.

"What is it?" I ask in a quiet voice.

"The girl in your vision, the one who was dead, has been found."

"Is it Kayla?" I ask, my voice breaking as I imagine my old friend dead.

"No. It was Elena."

"Oh." Even though I'm relieved that it's not Kayla, tears slip down my cheeks as I think of Elena.

"It was just like Michael's drawing. Really amazing, Samantha."

I'm crying now and I can't even speak.

"I know this must be hard for you," she says. "We're all feeling upset and sad, but we're also feeling encouraged. You were right on. Your vision really was a gift from God. You shouldn't—"

"But why did He show me too late? Why couldn't we have gotten to Elena sooner?"

"I don't know, Samantha. I don't know much about any of this yet. But the FBI agent I've been working with— his name is Tony—wants to meet you. He's very impressed with your—"

"But what about Kayla?" I demand through my tears. "What does this mean for her?" I use the back of my hand to wipe my nose. "Do you think she's dead too?"

"Like I said, I don't know. I'm sorry…we really don't know much yet. I'm waiting on Tony for more details. And I know this is upsetting for you to hear. I just thought you should know what was going on."

"I know...I know..." I try to get ahold of myself. "I'm sorry for getting mad at you, Ebony. It's not your fault. But it's just so frustrating."

"Trust me, I know how you feel. I really wanted to find Elena while she was still alive. I'm still hoping that we'll find Kayla—soon. I can't imagine why God would give you these specific dreams and visions if He doesn't want us to find her alive."

The image from my vision flashes through my mind's eye again—Elena lying in the dirt, dead and pale and lifeless, and I begin to cry even harder now. From the sweet-looking girl in the photo on the missing persons list, she appeared to be about my age, probably with a family who dearly loved her, and now she is dead. Probably tortured and beaten and God only knows what else before she died. It's just too much to absorb.

"Are you going to be okay, Samantha?" Ebony asks in a compassionate voice. "Are you home alone? Do you need to—?"

"I'm okay. Just a little shaken." I take in a quick, jagged breath. "It makes my head and my heart actually hurt just to think of Elena, you know, like that. And then Kayla..."

"I know..."

"But I appreciate you telling me. I'll be praying for Elena's family."

"Yes, this is hard news. Especially at Christmas."

I sink down onto my bed. "Yeah..."

"We might need your help, Samantha."

"What do you mean?"

"I mean Tony wants to talk to you."

"The FBI guy?"

"Yes. He's very interested in your work."

"My work?" I flop onto my back now, pushing my hair back and letting out a deep breath.

"Yes. I wasn't quite sure how to explain you to him. He sort of thinks that you work with us at the police department."

"Oh."

"Anyway, I know that it's almost Christmas, but I wondered if you'd be interested in flying down to Phoenix with me."

I sit up straight. "To Phoenix? When?"

"Well, I was thinking maybe tomorrow morning…"

"Tomorrow morning?" I'm trying to wrap my head around this. Ebony wants me to fly to Phoenix tomorrow? Like just three days before Christmas? "Why?"

"Tony thinks you can help them find Kayla."

"Oh."

"What do you think, Samantha?"

"I don't know… I mean, of course I *want* to find Kayla—more than anything. But I'm just not sure how I can help. It's not as if I control this thing, not any more than I can control God. Like you said, Ebony, I'm just the vessel."

"But you're willing?"

"Of course."

"Then, do you mind if I talk to your mom about this?"

"No, of course not." Although I know this may pose a problem since I cannot imagine Mom giving her blessing for me to go to Phoenix with Ebony on such short notice like this. And just a few days before Christmas too.

"Is she at work?"

I look at my watch. "Yeah, until about five I think she said."

"Okay. I'll keep you posted."

I hang up and replay what I've just heard, trying to sort out and make sense of it. Elena is dead. Kayla may still be alive. Tony from the FBI thinks I can help them to find her. Ebony wants me to fly down to Phoenix with her tomorrow. She's calling my mom right now. Then the biggest question hits me—what does God want?

I go straight to my knees, fully aware that only God can make something like this work out. Forgetting about my fashion challenge, tonight's "double date," and everything else about ordinary life, I focus my heart on God—I ask Him to work His will for this, to show Mom and me and Ebony what's best for everyone. And eventually I tell Him that I am His and that I am willing to do whatever He wills for me. "Just keep me in Your will," I finally pray. "All I want is to do what You want me to do. I trust You. Amen."

When I stand up and look around my room, I'm surprised to remember that only an hour ago, I was obsessing over what to wear tonight. It suddenly seems so juvenile, so superficial. It's nearly five now, and I'm guessing that Ebony has already called Mom. Or maybe she's talking to her right now. I'm tempted to call Olivia to tell her the whole story, but I want to be ready in case Ebony calls me back. I see my Bible sitting on my desk. It's flopped open to Proverbs right now, and I pick it up and begin to read, randomly, from the right-hand page.

> *Trust GOD from the bottom of your heart;*
> *Don't try to figure out everything on your*
> *own. Listen for GOD's voice in everything*
> *you do, everywhere you go; he's the one who*
> *will keep you on track. (Proverbs 3:5–6)*

Now, I realize this Scripture isn't like God's green light for me to head off to Phoenix with Ebony tomorrow, but it does give me a strong sense of peace. And if Mom agrees and I do go to Phoenix, it will be because it is God's will. And I'm thinking, if it's God's will to go to Phoenix, maybe it's also His will that we find Kayla. I just pray that we find her alive.

I jump when the phone rings, but this time it's the land line, and this time it's Olivia.

"Ready for the big night?" she asks in a cheerful voice.

"Uh, yeah, I guess…"

"What do you mean, *I guess*?" She sounds disappointed. "I thought you were looking forward to this, Samantha."

"I am. It's just that, well…" And then I tell her the latest news, about Elena and about Ebony's invitation for me to go to Phoenix.

"Man, that's so sad about Elena. I'd really been praying for her."

"I know, me too." I feel that spirit of depression coming over me again.

"And they know it's her, for sure?"

"I guess so. Ebony didn't give many details, but I'm pretty sure that rules out the possibility of it being Kayla."

"That's something to be thankful for. Still, it's so tragic for Elena and her family. So sad."

"Yeah, I'm pretty bummed." I let out a long sigh.

"Kind of puts a damper on our big night, huh?"

"I'm sorry, Olivia."

"Hey, it's not your fault, Sam."

"The truth is, I just really don't feel much like going out now."

"But what good would it do for you to sit at home and feel bad?"

"Yeah, I know…"

"What we need to do is pray, Samantha."

"I have been praying."

"Let's pray right now," she says. "Let's pray for Elena's family. Let's ask God to bring something good out of this tragedy. Okay?"

"Okay." Then I mostly listen while Olivia prays. Her faith feels like a life preserver that's been thrown out to me as I'm floundering in the waves, and by the time she says amen and I agree with her, I'm feeling hopeful again.

"Thanks," I tell her. "I needed that."

"Me too."

"It's hard to imagine how God can use something like this, but I guess that's where our faith comes in, huh?"

"Yeah," she says. "I guess so."

I look at my messy closet that I've recently ransacked in search of the perfect outfit. "Uh, do you mind if I just wear jeans tonight?"

"Nope. Not at all. Let's go for comfort."

"I better go," I tell her. "I hear my mom downstairs. I should go find out what she thinks about Ebony's travel plans for me."

"Good luck. I'll be praying."

We hang up, and I go down to see if I can read anything on my mom's face. But as she hangs up her coat and sets down her bag, she looks pretty much the same— slightly haggard but glad to be home.

"Hey, Mom," I say somewhat cautiously.

"Hi, Sam." She kicks off her shoes and flops down on the couch. "What a day."

"Want a soda?" I ask as I head for the fridge.

"No. I'm too cold already. It's nearly freezing outside. I've heard we might even get a little snow again."

"How about some tea?" I offer.

"Sure, that sounds great."

"Constant Comment?" I call out, knowing that's her favorite.

"Lovely."

Now, as I make us a pot of this sweet, spicy tea, I'm wondering if her relatively calm demeanor means that she's okay about my going to Phoenix, or does it mean that she said "Absolutely not" and is trying to be nice because she thinks I'll be disappointed. I decide not to say anything, just to play it out.

Mom's flipped on the news as I join her with our tea. "Thanks," she says as I hand her a mug. She takes a sniff. "Mmm, perfect."

I sit beside her, absently watching the news show on CNN.

"You still going to the movie with your friends?"

"Yeah. They'll be here in about an hour."

She smiles. "That's nice."

Okay, the curiosity is killing me, but I'm determined to wait for her to say something. Then I see a photo on TV that makes me nearly drop my mug of tea.

"Turn that up, will you?" I lean forward to peer at the same photo I picked out at the police station just a few days ago.

"The victim has been identified as nineteen-year-old Elena Maiesa," the woman reporter is saying, *"a second-year student at Arizona State. Maiesa was reported missing by friends shortly after classes began in September. Although no foul play was suspected at the time, according to our sources, Maiesa died of strangulation and may have been deceased for more than two weeks. No suspects have been disclosed as of this date, but police ask that anyone having any knowledge of this case contact them."* And just like that, they move on to the next story.

But I just sit there in shock. Somehow seeing it all in front of you, pictures of Elena and footage of the place where her body was found—well, it's totally unnerving.

Eighteen

"Are you okay?" my mom asks with a worried expression.

I just stare blankly at her, but my hands are shaking so much that I have to set my mug of tea on the coffee table before I spill it.

"You look like you just saw a ghost, Samantha."

I nod. "Yeah. I kind of feel like I did."

"What are you talking about?" She frowns at me. "Are you having some kind of a vision or something?"

"Did Ebony call you today?"

"Ebony?" She looks confused now.

"You know, the detective at the—"

"I know who she is. But why would she call me? Is something wrong with Zach? He didn't run away from the rehab place, did he? Or did the police find out something new? Was he more involved in the drug deal than we—?"

"No, it's not about Zach."

"What then? Why should Ebony call me?"

I take in a deep breath, silently asking God to lead me. I really didn't want to be the one to break this to Mom. "That girl on the news just now, Elena Maiesa…"

"The college girl who was murdered?"

"Yeah."

"Do you know her?"

"Sort of."

"Was she from Oregon? Did she live in town?"

"No, I never actually met her, but I had a dream, a week or so ago…she was in it."

"But you never met her?"

"No."

"Then how did you know it was her?" Mom is clearly confused now. And I can tell she's getting irritated too.

"It's a long story," I say quickly. "But I'll try to condense it. You already know that I was helping Ebony with Kayla's case. But then I had this dream about Elena, only I thought it was Kayla. But then I saw her face, and she obviously doesn't look anything like Kayla."

"Obviously." Mom scowls as she studies me.

"And then I had a vision, just a few days ago, only in this vision the girl was dead."

"Oh, Samantha." Mom closes her eyes and takes in a deep breath, and I can sense that she's disgusted with this—with me.

"I can't help it, Mom. It's not like I ask for these dreams and visions. They just come to me and I have to—"

"I think you should go see Paula again."

Paula is Mom's shrink-friend, the woman I went to see last year when Mom thought I was losing it. "I'm not crazy, Mom."

"But this is not normal, Samantha. Having visions about dead girls is not normal."

"What *is* normal?"

She sadly shakes her head as she wraps her hands around her mug of tea. "Sometimes I'm not too sure."

"Maybe this is normal for me," I say in what I hope is a calming tone. "Dad understood it. And Grandma McGregor would've understood it. Ebony even seems to understand it."

Mom narrows her eyes at me. "I suppose you wish Ebony was your mother."

"No, of course not. I just wish you could understand this. I wish you could accept—"

Just then the doorbell rings. "Is that your friends?"

"No, it's too early. But I'll get it." Eager to get out of this conversation, which seems to be going nowhere but down, and quickly, I go to see who's at the door. To my surprise, and huge relief, it's Ebony.

"Sorry to just show up like this," she says as I let her in, "but I tried and tried to reach your mom, and when I finally got through, they told me she'd gone home. Since I was already in my car, I thought I'd just pop in. Is that okay?"

"Of course. Come on in. Mom's in the family room." I call out to Mom, announcing that Ebony is here.

"Well, that's ironic." Mom waves to Ebony without getting up. "We were just talking about you. Well, sort of. Have a seat."

"Can I take your coat?" I offer, and Ebony hands me her pretty suede jacket, which I carefully hang over a chair.

"Sorry to just burst in here." Ebony sits next to my mom, "but I really need to talk to you, Beth." I'm surprised that Ebony is calling Mom by her first name now, but maybe this is something that transpired when she helped her with Zach last week.

"Is this about the girl who was murdered in Arizona?" my mom demands.

Ebony glances at me. "Samantha told you about that?"

"We just watched it on the news."

Ebony nods. "Yes. That's part of it."

"Well, I was just telling Samantha that I'm getting very concerned. This is not normal behavior for a sixteen-year-old—"

"Almost seventeen," I remind her. "Less than a month."

"Fine, seventeen-year-old girl. It's still not normal."

"I'm sure it must be confusing," says Ebony. "Gifts like this are hard for people to understand, but you have to respect that your daughter is special."

"Oh, I know she's special..." Mom sort of smiles. "And believe me, I'm grateful for her—especially in times like this, with Zach off in rehab and Cliff off in, well..." She sadly shakes her head. "Anyway, don't think I'm not thankful for my daughter. I most certainly am."

"Yes, I'm sure you are," Ebony assures her. "But it must be hard to accept that she has this very unusual gift for—"

"For having visions and dreams about *dead* or missing girls?" my mom interrupts, peering closely at Ebony's face as if she thinks there might be a clue there. "Don't you think that's just a little abnormal, not to mention downright weird? Don't you think that girls Samantha's age should be out having fun and doing normal teenage things? Instead of obsessing over missing girls and dead people? I was just telling Samantha that I think it's time she went back to talk to our psychologist friend, Dr. Paula Stone. Maybe she needs medication or some special kind of therapy."

"Oh, I don't think she's—"

"Who made you such an expert on my daughter?" Mom says in an overly loud voice. "Okay, fine, I know that you stepped in and helped us when it came to Zach. And it's not as if I don't appreciate that, Ebony. I do. But what makes you think you know so much about Samantha? Why are you dragging her into all this?"

Okay, I'm getting worried now. Mom is losing her cool again—something she doesn't normally do in front of others, although I'm remembering that she's done this before with Ebony. And suddenly I'm wondering if this has something to do with Ebony personally. She used to be Dad's partner, and she was there with him on that day, his backup when he got shot. Is this why Mom is being so hard on her? Or is it just about me?

Ebony's brows pull together slightly, and I can tell she's hurt, but she doesn't say anything.

"Mom," I begin in a pleading tone. "Ebony hasn't *dragged* me into anything. I'm the one who came to her in the first place. I'm the one who told her about my dreams and visions about Kayla. She's simply trying to do her job—trying to locate a missing girl who happens to be my friend. And I'm just trying to help her."

"Help her?" Mom echoes. "By having dreams about dead girls? How is that helping anyone? It seems like your involvement with the police is only taking you in deeper and deeper, Samantha. And trust me, if you go nuts on me and end up being locked up in some psych unit somewhere, the police won't be there for you. I'll be the one left to pick up the pieces—the police will just use you and lose you. Just like they did to your dad." And then she covers her face with her hands and bends over and just starts sobbing.

I look helplessly at Ebony. Like what do we do now? But Ebony just puts her hand on Mom's back and says soothingly, "It's okay, Beth. I understand. I know this is hard. But I do understand."

Well, I'm glad someone understands because, to be honest, I'm finding this whole thing totally overwhelming and confusing. Not to mention stressful. It's like Mom is this big mess of mixed-up emotions, like a tangled kite string that is so knotted and twisted that I don't see how she'll ever figure it out. Seriously, if someone in this family needs counseling, well, besides Zach, I think it's Mom.

Still, I know that I should have compassion. "I'm sorry, Mom," I tell her as she continues to cry. "I wish you could understand that I'm okay. I know that God has given me this gift. I know that He won't hurt me with it. And He won't let the police hurt me either. I'm not worried, and I wish that you weren't."

She sits up now and just looks at me.

"You're carrying a heavy load, Beth. You shouldn't be carrying it alone."

"But I am alone," she says in a hardened tone. "You should know that better than anyone." She glares at Ebony now. "You were there when it happened."

Ebony glances uncomfortably at me, and I strongly suspect this is a conversation that should happen between the two of them. This is not something I really want to participate in.

"I'm going to a movie with friends tonight." I glance at my watch. "And they'll be here in about fifteen minutes. I really need to get ready if you don't—"

"Go," Mom says, waving her hand. "At least that's a fairly normal thing for a teenager to do."

Ebony nods. "Yes. And have fun, Samantha."

So I make my escape, praying for both of them as I hurry up the stairs to my room. I know this won't be easy, but I suspect it's something that needs to happen for my mom's sake. I feel resolved as far as Ebony goes—as far as her involvement in the last day of my dad's life. I trust her completely. Hopefully Mom can reach that same place. Maybe she can even begin to untangle all the messy strings that seem wrapped around her heart.

I'm barely ready to go when I hear a car pull up in the driveway. Although I'd like for Mom to meet Conrad, I don't think this is the time for it. So I just tell her good-bye and when I'll be home; then I dash out the door just as Conrad comes up the walk.

"Hey, I was coming up to get you. I thought I should meet your mom, you know?"

"That's okay," I tell him, noticing that Alex is getting into the backseat now. "She's kind of tied up with someone else at the moment. Maybe I can introduce you to her later."

"Everything okay?"

"Sort of." Then I see the concern in his eyes. "Actually, my mom is having kind of a rough time of it tonight. It has to do with losing my dad and stuff."

"I'm sorry," he says as he opens the passenger door to his funny little Gremlin car to let me in. Alex is grinning at me from the backseat.

"Hey," I say as I get in. "How's it going, Alex?"

"I'm cool. But it's a little cozy back here."

"You want to sit in the front?" I offer.

"Nah, I'm fine."

Soon we have Olivia, but before we leave her house, Conrad turns to me. "I can tell you're worried about your mom, Samantha. Do you think we should pray for her?"

I'm really surprised but touched by his offer. "That'd be so great." Then without going into too many details, I quickly explain what's going on to Alex. "I don't think she ever really got over losing my dad. And his old partner from the force, well, she's a Christian and a pretty cool lady. I just hope she can help my mom to move on, you know?"

"I still remember hearing about it," says Alex. "I didn't really know you back then, well, other than that you went to our church. But I remember feeling really bad for you guys."

"Yeah, we all did," says Conrad. And then he leads us in a very perceptive prayer for my mom, and I can't believe how blessed I am to be with such cool friends tonight.

"Thanks," I tell them. "You have no idea how much that means to me."

And then we're talking about the movie we're about to see, remembering some things from the last movie and discussing how it differed slightly from the books and what we did or didn't like about it. And I'm thinking, this is what dating (if that's what you call this) should be like—just friends hanging together and having a good time. And I'd think that my mom would be happy for me and that she'd consider this to be fairly "normal" behavior for an almost seventeen-year-old girl. At least I hope so.

The movie turns out to be pretty good, but I have to admit that I was distracted—too much going on—and I promise myself to rent it on DVD when it comes out. Afterward, we go out for pizza, and I do my best to act like a "normal" girl, but more and more I'm wondering if perhaps Mom is right. Maybe I am abnormal, a misfit, a girl on the verge of losing it. Still, I keep these thoughts to myself. No need to spoil everyone's evening.

Finally, our big night comes to an end. But when we're back at Olivia's house—the first drop-off—Conrad asks if we should pray again. "I sense that you're still having a hard time with this, Samantha."

"I'm sorry," I tell him. "I was trying to wear my happy face. Was it that obvious?"

"It's okay," Olivia assures me from the backseat. "I know you're going through some hard stuff right now. Why don't you just let the three of us pray for you this time?"

I sigh deeply. "That'd probably be good."

And so I just sit there as the three of them pray for me. Most of their prayers seem related to my mom and getting over the loss of my dad, but I sense a very real spirit of caring and compassion, and I am deeply moved when they're finally done.

"Thank you so much!" I tell them. "You guys are a total blessing to me!"

Finally, we're at my house, and Conrad is walking me to the door (just as Alex walked Olivia to her door), which makes this feel more like a date than ever. And okay, I know it's crazy, but suddenly I'm all nervous, like is he going to kiss me or something? And I am so totally not ready for that. But instead he just takes my hand and gives it a little shake. "I had a cool time tonight, Samantha. Thanks for going out with me."

I smile in relief. "Me too. Thanks for taking me."

"So, maybe you're not completely opposed to dating?"

I shrug. "I guess it all depends on how you define dating. But what happened tonight was awesome, Conrad. Despite the crud going on at home, I had a good time."

"Cool." He nods. "And I hope things get better with your mom."

"Thanks. I'll let you know how it goes." Part of me really wishes I could tell him about everything—about

Ebony and Kayla and Elena and Phoenix, but I know that it's something I need to keep undercover.

I mean, maybe he would understand. But it would also greatly complicate my life. And just like the verse where Jesus tells us to do our good deeds in secret, I believe that God wants me to keep this side of my life private too. And that's okay. I can live with that.

Nineteen

It's hard to believe that I'm actually flying to Phoenix right now. Ebony is seated next to me, eyes closed, and I'm not sure if she's dozing or praying as our plane finally taxis to the runway. Our flight was delayed for more than two hours, and everyone was getting pretty antsy. "Too much holiday traffic," was the excuse, but I also overheard someone talking about "mechanical troubles."

So feeling a little uneasy myself, just as the plane speeds up to take off, I tightly shut my eyes and pray for a safe flight. Then I grasp the arms of the seat and watch out the window as the Portland airport falls away and then gets smaller and smaller. I watch as we circle over the Columbia River, trying not to imagine what it would feel like to land in the gray icy water below.

The flight attendant told us there were life vests under our seats, but I didn't pay close attention to how to use them in an "actual emergency." Then I ask myself, if this flight was really going down, wouldn't God have shown me in advance? Or maybe not.

I've flown a couple of times before—once to Disneyland with my family, and once with just Zach and me when we went to visit Grandma Martha (my mom's mom) in Seattle for about a month during the summer that Mom went back to college. But it still makes me nervous to be thirty-five thousand feet above the earth with only some plastic and metal between us and thin air. Still, I remind myself to trust God. My life is in His hands.

And then to further distract myself, I focus on Kayla, praying for her and that we'll get down there in time—to find her, alive. I was pretty surprised that Mom agreed to let me go to Arizona with Ebony. When I left them last night, I wasn't sure what I'd return home to. But to my relief, Mom was acting pretty normal when I got home.

"Did you have a good time?" she asked when I came tiptoeing into the house, halfway hoping that she'd already gone to bed and that I could slip to my room without another encounter.

"Yeah. The movie was pretty good."

"Want some cocoa?" she offered, and I could see she had the ingredients all ready to go, as if she'd been expecting me. She was wearing her old blue bathrobe, the same one she's had since I was little.

"Sure," I said with surprise, since my mom hasn't been particularly domestic or nurturing these past few years. But hey, I'll take what I can get when I can get it. I sat on a stool by the island and watched as she proceeded to make cocoa the old-fashioned way—the way she used to when Dad was still alive. She poured milk into the pan, measured in powdered baking cocoa and sugar and just a few drops of vanilla, then set it on the stove to heat. I became almost mesmerized as she stirred the spoon round and round, making a dull metallic dinging sound each time it hit the sides of the pan.

"Sorry I fell apart this afternoon," she said as she finally skimmed the skinlike surface of the cocoa into the sink. Then she poured the remaining steaming contents into a couple of big stoneware mugs, added some marshmallows, then handed one mug to me with a sad little half smile.

"That's okay," I told her as she sat across from me.

"Well, no…" she said slowly. "It's not okay."

"Okay…"

"I had no right to treat Ebony like that. Or you either."

"You were stressed out, Mom."

"I was mad."

"Oh." I sigh. "At me?"

Mom shook her head as she blew on her cocoa. "No, I was mad at Ebony. I was blaming her…for everything, I think. I know it makes no sense, but Ebony was becoming the focus of all my problems. I was making her into the devil."

"Ebony?" I said in disbelief, ready to defend my good friend but knowing I should just be quiet and listen.

"I think I've blamed her for your father's death right from the start. Oh, I never would've admitted this to anyone. It would've sounded so bitter, so vindictive. But I think I've held her responsible all along, Samantha."

I didn't know what to say. So I said nothing, just kept sipping my cocoa.

"Right after it happened, I overheard some police friends of your dad's talking at the precinct. I'd gone in to pick up some of his things and to sign some papers, but I heard an officer saying that Ebony blew it, that if she'd been more experienced and had reacted differently and hadn't been a woman…well, that your dad never would've been killed."

"Oh."

"And then here this woman is," Mom continued, "back in my life. First she's trying to take over my daughter, and the next thing she's getting my son carted off to rehab— and I know that was a good thing, Samantha, believe me, I know that. But it was just so strange. And I was really starting to resent that woman. A lot."

"That makes sense."

"In a crazy way."

"So did you talk to her about this?"

She nodded and took a slow sip. "I asked her to tell me about what happened that day—the day Dad was shot…"

"I asked her the same thing," I told Mom. "The very first time we talked."

"Well, I guess I should've asked her sooner."

"So, she told you?"

"Yes. And it makes sense. I can imagine your dad doing just as she said, telling the less-experienced cop to stand aside and going down the narrow staircase alone, without even calling for backup, not really expecting to find anything much. He was taken by surprise, Samantha. I suppose if anyone made a mistake that day, it was him." She wiped a straggler tear from her cheek. "But I needed to hear it from Ebony. I needed to sort of clean the slate with her."

I let out a sigh. "So, you're okay with her now?"

She nodded. "And now it seems that Ebony wants to take you to Phoenix with her."

I cringed inwardly, unsure of where this would go. "She told you about that?"

Mom nodded again. "It's amazing, Samantha. I don't really understand it, and it worries me. But she said your vision about that Hispanic girl who was murdered was right on the money."

"Yeah, right on but too late."

"But Ebony thinks it's related to Kayla. And I suppose if you can help Kayla, if you can keep her from ending up like—like that other poor girl—then who am I to stand in your way?"

"Really?" I said in total shock. "I can go?"

"I made Ebony swear on her own life and her mother's that nothing would happen to you, Samantha. I told her that I would never forgive her, or myself for that matter, if anything happened to you. I couldn't take it."

I wanted to point out to her that only God could keep a promise like that, but didn't want to push it too hard with my mom. She'd already been through a lot.

"Thanks, Mom," I said as I finished my cocoa. "And I know that God is watching out for me. So I hope you won't worry."

"Your flight is noonish," she told me. "Ebony will be here to get you around nine. She wanted to get an early start since it's the holidays and the airport is supposedly a mess."

"I'll be ready," I told her, going around to the other side to give her a big hug. "And you won't be sorry, Mom."

Mom frowned. "I hope not."

I hope not too as we fly across the state. So much seems to be riding on this trip. I don't want to disappoint anyone. Then I remind myself that it's not on my shoulders, but God's. He's the one who'll have to do the directing. I just need to lean on Him. And trust.

The sun is just going down when we arrive in Phoenix. A short, dark Hispanic man, who turns out to be Tony Mendez from the FBI, meets us at passenger pick up, and since we have no checked bags, we go straight out to his car, where despite the dusky sky, it feels like it's about 100 degrees.

"Man, it's hot," I say as I climb into the backseat of a dark-colored SUV.

"Yeah, especially for this time of year," he admits from the front, where Ebony is seated next to him. "It's been in the nineties. Usually it's more like the seventies."

This reminds me of my dreams and how it was stifling in that little dark room, where I could barely move and breathe.

"There are some bottles of water back there," he says. "Help yourself. It's easy to get dehydrated down here."

So I take one and hand one to Ebony, thankful for the cool wetness.

"I'm going to take you directly to your hotel. I was hoping we'd get started on this today, but your flight

was so late that I don't think it's worth it to start looking yet."

I'm not sure what he means by "looking," but I decide
to just listen.

"Still, I'd like to ask you some questions, Samantha. Kind
of a debriefing, you know? And I'd like to compare notes
with you, Detective Hamilton. I'll drop you off, and you can
check in and drop off your things then meet me downstairs at the restaurant to talk and have some dinner.
Sound okay?"

"Sounds fine," she tells him.

It's almost seven o'clock by the time we reconvene in
the hotel restaurant, but Tony is patiently waiting next to an
enormous Christmas tree. It seems totally weird that we're
in this warm, sunny place and it's almost Christmas, but
as we walk out to a table by the pool, I hear a jazzy version of "White Christmas" playing over the sound system.
It feels like I've entered the holiday *Twilight Zone.*

Tony makes small talk, letting us finish our meals before
he starts in on the more serious questions. He begins by
asking me about how well I knew Kayla and what I thought
of her and why she took off like that and then slowly works
his way into how it was that I got my "information."

"It's kind of hard to explain." I glance at Ebony. "And
some people don't really understand, but it's a gift from
God." I wait for his response, but he just nods and jots
something down in his little notebook. "I've had it since I
was a little kid, and I guess my paternal grandmother, who
is deceased, had it too. Sometimes I have these dreams,

kind of prophetic dreams, you know? And sometimes I have visions." Then I tell him the verse my dad told me that's from Joel in the Old Testament.

"I see..."

"Really?" I question him. "Or are you just being nice?"

He grins. "You know, I've been in the FBI for about twenty-seven years now, Samantha. I've seen a lot of things that are tough to explain. But I do believe in God. So why couldn't He do something like this?"

I try not to show my surprise. "Right..."

Then he asks me more questions, specifically about my visions and dreams, taking notes the whole time while I talk. And finally he says, "Okay, now tell me, what is your gut feeling about this, Samantha? Do you think that Elena Maiesa and Kayla Henderson were somehow connected? Or do you think you might've just gotten your spiritual wires crossed, so to speak?"

I carefully consider this. "I do think they're connected."

"Why?"

"I can't even explain it, but it's like you said. It's a gut feeling."

He nods. "Okay, I can go with that. I just needed to hear it from the horse's mouth." He's studying his notes now. "So you had this dream about Elena Maiesa being dead just a week or so ago? Is that right?"

I have to think about this. So much has happened that it seems like a long time ago, but I know it wasn't. "Not even a week," I finally say. "And it wasn't a dream. It was a vision." I describe the billboard and what I saw; then

Ebony mentions the composite drawing that Michael cre-
ated from it.

"Yes," says Tony. "That was instrumental in finding the
Maiesa girl." He shakes his head sadly. "Right down to
the shoe."

"The shoe?" I echo.

"Yes. It was there at the site. And since we didn't have
any way to immediately identify the victim, we contacted
the family, and they confirmed that Elena had a pair of
shoes fitting that description."

"So sad..." I say as I remember the lone Adidas shoe
with the blue stripes all covered with dust.

"Does it make you wonder?" muses Tony. "I mean,
why you'd have a vision of a girl, but she'd already been
dead for nearly two weeks by then? Why didn't you have
this vision *before* she died?"

"I wondered that exact thing, and it was pretty discour-
aging. But it's times like that when I have to trust God. Like
Ebony keeps reminding me, I don't have control over this
thing any more than I have control over God." I stir my
iced tea and think about this. "But I think that's one more
reason that Elena is connected to Kayla."

"How's that?"

"I think God showed me what happened to Elena,
even though it was after the fact, just so it doesn't happen
to Kayla."

"I hope you're right."

Then Tony explains that the plan is to start out first thing
in the morning. "You'll probably want to hit the hay early;

we'd like to be out on the road as soon as the sun comes up. We'll begin with the site where Elena was found." He glances nervously at Ebony, as if he's worried about me. "It's cleaned up, of course, but I'm hoping the location itself will stir something up for Samantha. Maybe God will give her a vision or something. We've collected a lot of evidence and have some clues, but that's about it." He turns and looks at me. "Other than your composite drawing of this Colby character, whom no one seems to have seen, we don't have a clear suspect yet."

"Well, I'll really be praying tonight," I tell him. "I'll ask God to help us."

"Me too," says Tony.

"I'm with you," agrees Ebony. Then we tell Tony good night and head to our room. "I hope you don't mind rooming with me," she says as we go inside the large room with two queen-size beds. "But I promised your mom that I would keep an eye on you."

"Not at all. I'd probably feel uncomfortable being in a room by myself anyway."

"Well, I'm exhausted," she says. "But if you want to watch TV or anything, feel free."

I admit that I'm tired too, and we both are in bed before ten o'clock. But as soon as the lights are out and it's quiet, other than the street noise down below, I am wide awake. Finally, after tossing and turning for nearly an hour, I get up and go sit by the window, just looking out, although there's not much to see down there besides the pool and other parts of the hotel that wrap around it.

It's my first time in Arizona, and I try to imagine how Kayla must've felt coming here. Where did she go? What did she see? Where did she stay? It's about midnight when I return to bed, so tired that I'm asleep before I know it.

I've made a huge mistake," I say to the man who's approaching me now, too fast and too deliberately. We're out in the desert, trying to find the site where Elena was killed, but somehow I've gotten separated from the others. And now I'm in trouble. Big-time trouble.

I'm slowly backing away from this guy, glancing over my shoulder for a place to escape to but knowing there is nowhere to run. Only the wall of the building behind me. Why did I let myself get into this position? Why am out here all by myself with this horrible, evil man? I can feel his evil—seeping from his oversized pores—as he moves closer toward me.

"Take it easy, sugar," he says in a voice that's tinged with a southern accent. "I ain't gonna hurt you. Just let me explain everything nice and slow and easy. Okay?"

"I just want you to leave me alone," I say in what I hope is a firm I-mean-business sort of voice. "I've made a mistake, and I just want to leave now."

The guy looks vaguely familiar to me, but I'm sure we've never met before. His face is ruddy and pudgy, and his eyes are small and pale and slightly close together. Kind of a pig face, although I wouldn't dare say this. I already

Twenty

221

know that I've offended him simply by trying to get away from him.

"Just calm yourself down, little girl," he tells me, still approaching, now only a couple feet away. "I know I'm not exactly what you expected to find here, but you'll like me...once you get to know me. I'll be your sugar daddy, and you'll be my baby. I'll be good and sweet to you, just as long as you are good and sweet to me, doll face."

And now I am flat against the wall. Through my T-shirt, I can feel the coolness of cement blocks pressed against my back. It would be a relief in this hot dry air, except that I know I'm trapped.

"Please," I beg this horrible man, "just leave me alone." But he continues moving closer. So close now that I can smell the body odor emanating from his sweaty blue T-shirt.

"I made a mistake," I say again. "I didn't mean to come here."

He leans forward, and his hot stinky breath, a combination of sour milk and stale tobacco, makes me want to gag as he plants both of his hands on either side of my shoulders. "Just relax, sugar. I ain't gonna hurt you."

I raise my arms, double my fists, and begin to scream and flail against him, begging this monster to go away. *"Leave me alone!"*

"Samantha!"

He's shaking me now—but when I open my eyes, all I see is Ebony. She's standing over me, still in her silk pajamas, but looking down at me with real concern. My heart is racing so fast that it feels like it's about to separate itself from my chest.

"Oh, Ebony!" I cry in frightened relief. "It was a dream! *A really bad dream!*" I'm trembling, and it feels like I can barely breathe as she wraps her arms around me, patting me on the back, rocking me from side to side.

"It's okay. Just relax and breathe. You're all right now, Samantha. Take a deep breath. *Relax.* You're in the hotel room with me. You're safe."

Finally I'm calm enough that I'm able to talk, and I tell her about the terrifying dream.

"Do you think it was Colby?" she asks when I'm finished.

"Yeah. I didn't realize it in my dream, or not at first any-way. I mean, he looked familiar, but at the same time I'd never seen him. I remember feeling confused, and for some reason I kept telling him that I'd made a mistake."

"I'll say." She shakes her head. "Well, don't worry, Samantha. There's no way we'll let you anywhere near that man."

"It was so awful, so freaky. I don't think I've ever felt that scared before. That must've been how Kayla felt…and Elena too."

"No one should have to go through something like that." She sits on her bed and folds her arms across her chest. "Not even in a dream." Then she looks at the clock on the bedside table. "I'm going to get up now. You go ahead and sleep in a little more if you want."

"Like I even can now." I push the twisted covers away from me.

Before long, we've both showered and have eaten our room service breakfast and are waiting by the front door for Tony Mendez to come get us.

"This is Willie and Kevin." He nods to the two men in a similar SUV parked behind him. "They'll be our backup, just in case." He winks at Ebony. "Good to be prepared. And we've got more available if we need it."

Ebony waits until we're in the car with Tony before she informs him of my latest dream. Then Tony asks me to go over it in detail as he drives us out of town and onto a highway. Ebony takes notes, for the second time.

"So this creep in your dream looked like the man in the composite drawing?" asks Tony. "The Colby character?"

"Yes. But I didn't really get that at first. And he wasn't wearing the apron that said *Colby* on it."

"And that building you backed into?" he continues. "Did you get a look at it?"

I consider this. "You know, I think maybe I did actually see it, like earlier in my dream. I think it's the first thing that I saw actually. Let me try to remember…" I close my eyes and lean back, wishing that Michael Taylor were here to coach me. Then it comes to me. "Yes!" I say suddenly. "The building is what started the whole thing. I was walking in the desert; it seemed like we'd been hunting for the place where Elena's body was found, although that doesn't make sense since you know where it is. Anyway, I was walking and I was hot and I discovered this building, but it didn't really look like a building since it was really short and low to the ground, you know? Like probably just a bit taller than I am. I guess I thought it was maybe a place for animals or something. It was made of cement blocks that were painted; I remember the feeling of peeling paint on it. I think it was like a tannish color because it kind of blended in with the dirt. And I was walking toward this building when the man came up from behind me, and I turned around. That's when the dream got really vivid—and scary."

They're both quiet in the front seat, and suddenly I'm concerned that something is wrong. Or maybe I'm just not being very clear. "Does that make any sense?"

"Yes," says Tony. "It makes a lot of sense. But I guess that's why I'm feeling worried."

"Why?" I ask.

"Well, these dreams you have, sometimes they're prophetic, right?"

"Sometimes…"

"Well, what if your dream was some kind of a warning for you personally, Samantha?"

"Yes," says Ebony quickly. "I was just thinking the same thing."

"Huh?"

Ebony turns around in the front seat and looks at me with concerned eyes. "What if you're in danger by coming out here with us?"

"But why?" I ask.

"I don't know *why*," she says. "I mean, you're *with* us. Tony has backup. We're all armed. I honestly don't see how anything could possibly go wrong. "

"But that dream worries me," admits Tony.

"And I promised your mother that I'd protect you."

"And I'm sure you will." I remember my initial surprise this morning when I saw Ebony strapping on her handgun, now hidden beneath her white linen jacket. But then I realized that's part of her job.

"But that dream." Tony slows down now, like he's looking for a pullout, and I'm getting worried that he's going to turn around and take me back to the hotel. "What if it was for you, Samantha?"

"I don't think it was," I try to sound assuring. "Honestly, you guys, I think I was just walking in Kayla's shoes, you know? I've had dreams like that before where I feel what she feels and see what she sees. At least I assume that's what's happening. I guess I won't know for sure until…"

"But I don't want to put you in danger," Ebony says firmly.

"I really don't think I'm in danger," I say with confidence. "Honestly, I think God gave me that dream so I can show you something today. Maybe you'll even catch this Colby creep."

Tony glances at Ebony. "What do you think, Detective?"

Ebony turns fully around now, looking me straight in the eyes. "Are you certain, Samantha?"

I sort of shrug. "Who can be certain of anything? Besides God, that is?"

"I'm calling for more backup." Tony reaches for his phone.

"Thanks," says Ebony.

"And would you mind repeating the description of that setting over the phone for me, Samantha? I want someone back at the office to see if they can track down where a little building like that might possibly be located."

"No problem."

After Tony puts in his request for more backup, he hands the phone to me, and I tell a woman named Virginia about what I saw in my dream. "And you say the cement blocks were cool to the touch?" she asks after I'm done.

"Yes."

"Do you know what time of day it was?"

I think about this. "It seemed really bright out. Like it was midday. But I don't know for sure." She asks a couple more questions then thanks me and hangs up.

Now I look out the window and am amazed to see the mountains. "Those look like the mountains that Michael drew in his landscape composite," I tell Ebony with excitement. "Just like the ones in my vision."

"Yep," says Tony. "We're getting warmer."

"It seems like it should be easy to find that building," I say hopefully. "And maybe that will lead us to Colby and possibly to Kayla."

"It *seems* that way." Tony sighs. "But the fact is, there is a lot of country out here. And so much of it looks exactly the same. You could drive for days in circles and never find what you're looking for."

"Oh…"

So I sit back in my seat, enjoying the air-conditioning as I watch the desert scenery passing by. But as I sit here, I pray. I beg God to break through; I beg Him to show me something specific—something that will help us find Kayla.

Finally, after turning down a series of gravel then dirt roads that feel like a maze I would never find my way out of, Tony comes to a stop near an old, gnarly-looking tree. "This is it, ladies."

The other SUV is right behind us, and we all wait for the dust to settle before getting out. And when we get out, the air is quiet and still, and although it's only nine-thirty, it's already getting pretty warm outside.

"Take your time," Tony says to me in a quiet voice. "Just walk around and see if anything comes to you. But don't go past the taped-off sections. We still need to protect the crime scene in case we need to collect more evidence."

"I'm going to walk along with you," says Ebony. "But I won't say a word. I just don't want you getting more than a foot or two away from me. Especially after that dream you had."

So I walk around with Ebony by my side, and I try to feel something—something beyond the sadness, that is. Mostly I experience this heavy sense of gloom that seems to hang thickly in the air. Finally I stop and sit on a big rock that's partially shaded by the twisted old tree, which looks to be about a thousand years old.

I just sit here and try to imagine how this must've felt for Elena. What went on here? Was she already dead when he dumped her? Or did he kill her here? I could've asked Tony these questions, but now I just run the scenarios through my head and wonder. As I'm sitting here, wondering and pondering and trying to remain tuned in to God, I notice something like a hill off to my left. Of course, there are lots of small hills and rock formations all over the place, so I'm not sure why this one is any more notable than another, but for some reason it catches and holds my attention.

"What's over there?" I call out to where Tony and the others are standing around by the vehicles.

Tony walks over and asks what I'm talking about.

I point to the hill over there. "What's that?"

"That ridge?"

"Yeah."

He shrugs. "It's just a ridge, I guess. Why?"

"I just have this feeling about it. Like it's familiar or something."

"Did you see it in one of your visions or dreams?" he asks hopefully.

"Not that I can actually remember, but sometimes I don't remember every little thing. Like the dream last night. I didn't remember, at first, how I got to the place where I was backed up against that wall, you know?"

He peers over at the ridge, which I must admit looks rather unremarkable. "I don't see any road or trail heading that way. And we already scoured the place for tire tracks or footprints leading from the site. All we came up with were ones that lead back to the way we just came."

"So how do we get over there?" I persist.

He motions over to the other guys, who come to join us. "How would you get to that ridge over there?" he asks them.

Kevin shades his eyes as he peers at the ridge. "I'm not sure. I suppose you could get there on foot, but it'd take a while. We could try some of the other back roads, see if anything cuts back in there."

"You lead the way," says Tony, and we all head back to the SUVs. "Kevin grew up around here," he tells us as we buckle up. "He knows this country better than any of us. But even he admits that it's easy to get lost out here." Tony pats a device on his dashboard. "That's why we all rely on our trusty Global Positioning System."

We drive and drive, following a cloud of dust from the SUV in front of us as they try different roads, then turn around and go back. Seriously, if Tony hadn't shown me that GPS, I'd be certain we were lost. And then finally we go down a dirt road that takes us right up to a ridge. I'm relieved to get out of the SUV since I was starting to feel carsick.

"Does this look like it?" asks Tony.

I frown as I look up at the scraggly ridge. "I'm not really sure."

"Well, take your time," he says. "Look around."

We all start sort of nosing around, searching for…what? I'm not even sure. But as before, Ebony stays by my side as I walk and look and think. But I'm feeling confused and like I've led everyone on a wild-goose chase, like I'm just wasting their time.

"I just don't know…" I say to Ebony as I continue to walk aimlessly. "I'm not even sure why the ridge seemed important anymore."

"That's okay," she assures me. "It doesn't hurt to look around. I was getting tired of riding in the car anyway." She looks up at the sky. "Boy, it feels like it's about ninety degrees out here. I'm thirsty. You want a bottle of water too?"

"Yeah, thanks." I sit on another rock and just look blankly around, wondering why I thought that ridge meant anything. Then I see something that stops me, although it's not even in the general direction where we've all been looking, close to the ridge. This is off to the other side. It's just another one of those twisted old desert trees, but this one is sheared off and split at the top. I'm guessing it was hit by lighting, probably a long, long time ago.

Now, I know that it's most likely nothing, but for some reason it interests me, so I go closer and take a better look. And when I'm almost to the tree, I'm surprised to see that it's on the edge of another ridge, and the land behind it dips straight down, about ten or twelve feet, I'd estimate. I walk over to the ledge and look over, but I don't really see anything unusual. Just lots of rocks and sagebrush and cacti and a few gnarly trees.

I'm about to turn back when I notice that some of the rocks on this ledge form what could almost be a natural stairway going down. And I decide to try a few careful steps, wondering if the stones will hold or crumble. But they seem to hold, and I'm thinking this is just the sort of place my dad would've loved to hike and explore around in.

I take a few more cautious steps down, then pause and look back over to where the cars are parked, waving to Ebony as she comes my way with our bottles of water.

Before I know it, I'm down on this lower level. While it's interesting in a geological way, I don't see anything of real interest. I'm about to go back up when I hear a sound.

Suddenly I remember Tony's warning to watch out for snakes that might be sleeping in shady niches of rocks, and I jump away from the rock staircase, worried that I might've disturbed a rattler. But as I move I see something that's even more frightening than a rattlesnake—I see a short cement block building tucked into the back of this ridge, and it's painted in a peeling tan-colored paint. My heart is pounding as I look up to the top of the low ridge, expecting to see Ebony coming down the rocky trail, but she's not there.

My heart is pounding like a jackhammer now, and fully expecting to come face-to-face with the repulsive man from my dream last night, I am ready to run for my life. But I don't know which way to go—left or right or back up the rock stairs?

I feel certain that this monster must be directly behind me right now and that, if I turn around, I'll see his vile pig face smiling at me—maybe just a few feet away! And then to get away from him, I'll go backward. And I will back straight into the building, just like in my dream.

And I will be trapped!

Twenty-one

Instead of making the same mistake that I made in my dream, allowing myself to become trapped against the building, I take in a deep breath, pray a quick prayer, and let out the biggest, loudest, wildest scream that I've ever made in my entire life.

I just keep screaming and screaming like that until first Ebony and then the others scramble down the rocky staircase toward me. As soon as Ebony is at the bottom, I run to her, and only then do I turn around to see if Colby is lurking behind me. But to my amazed relief he's not.

"What?" says Ebony, breathlessly. Her gun is drawn and ready, as are the others', prepared for anything as the four of them huddle protectively around me.

I nod over to my left, to the building that's hidden beneath the ledge. *"It's right there!"* I whisper. *"The building in my dream!"*

They look slightly unconvinced, and I can't blame them since nothing appears to be there but a pile of stones that have tumbled down the ledge over the centuries. But with guns still drawn and ready, Ebony and the FBI agents slowly move around to a perspective where they can see what I've just seen.

I wait, barely daring to breathe, trying to remember exactly what I saw that set me to screaming. And suddenly I start to wonder if perhaps I just imagined the whole thing. Perhaps I'm suffering heatstroke or having hallucinations or am in need of the counseling services of Dr. Paula Stone once again.

But I can tell by their expressions and quick move-ments, as they get themselves into position, that all is not well. Then I hear Tony's hushed voice on his radio, calling for more backup.

I must've been right after all.

Ebony is back to my side in a flash, her left arm protec-tively wrapped around me as she looks in every direction. With handgun still firmly in hand, she slowly backs us up against a boulder, making a quiet shushing sound to me as she does so.

Every hair on my neck is standing on end now, and my knees are shaking so hard that I'm certain I'll collapse if Ebony should let go of me.

"Open up!" yells a man's voice. *"Police!"* This is fol-lowed by a loud bang and a thud, which I suspect is someone kicking down a door.

Then I hear muffled voices and some yelling, and the sharp sound of several gunshots stings my ears.

I jump, clinging even more tightly to Ebony, terrified that Tony or the other agents may have been shot or injured. What will we do?

It's the longest five minutes of my life as I stand here with Ebony, waiting to see the outcome of this thing, but finally Tony is back with us.

"We got the creep," he says, his dark eyes shining with excitement. "And the girl is in there. She's okay."

"Can we go to her?" I ask.

He nods. "Yes, please do; she looks terrified."

Ebony and I rush around the corner, where we see Kevin and Willie standing over a man who's sitting on the ground, his hands cuffed behind his back. I quickly look away. I don't want to see that face—I just want to forget him.

Then we hurry toward the short block building that I can now see has been built right into the side of the ridge, and with the stones piled over the roof, it is very camouflaged, very easy to miss.

The door is wide open now, and there, on a decrepit mattress on the floor, sits Kayla with her knees pulled up to her chin. She has on a dirty T-shirt and a pair of boxer style shorts. She looks stunned and ghostly pale, perhaps even in a state of shock.

"Kayla!" I kneel beside her and wrap my arms around her. "You're alive! You're safe!"

She looks even more bewildered when she realizes it's me. "Samantha?" she says in a hoarse-sounding voice. "Samantha McGregor?"

I nod.

"What are *you* doing here?"

"It's a long story, but you're safe now, Kayla."

Then she collapses onto my shoulder and just sobs and sobs like she may never stop crying again.

Soon Kayla and I are in the backseat of an air-conditioned SUV, where she is drinking a bottle of water and Tony is retracing the maze of dirt roads to get us back to the highway. The sheriff and medical assistance are on their way, but Tony felt we'd make better time to meet them.

"I was so stupid," she tells me, her voice still hoarse, I'm guessing from dehydration. "So incredibly, freakingly stupid…" Then she goes on to tell me about how she'd been communicating with this guy she'd met online through one of those weird matchmaker websites.

"I only did it to make Emma believe I had a boyfriend, so she would think I didn't care about Parker anymore. It started out as kind of a joke, you know? But this guy sounded so totally amazing in his e-mail…he was so mature, and his life sounded so awesome, his car, his condo…he told me there was an Olympic-size swimming pool. And his photograph…he looked so hot, so handsome…I honestly thought I was in love, Samantha. Can you believe it?"

I sigh. "You were tricked."

"Back then it seemed like Mom and me were fighting nonstop…and then I'd open up my e-mail, and there would be my dream guy saying all the right things. He told me that he loved me and that he wanted to take care of me. I thought he was my answer…my escape…*so stupid*!"

"He lied and manipulated you."

"But I came here of my own free will. Like a total idiot, I walked right into Colby's horrid little trap." Then she makes this awful face, and I'm afraid she's going to throw up.

"You okay?"

She takes in a quick breath and another swig of water. "I just can't stand to say his name. It makes me want to hurl. *I hate him so much!*"

"Don't think about him. Just be thankful that you're okay."

"I can't believe you guys found me." She peers at me curiously now. "But I don't understand why *you're* here, Samantha."

"Well, you remember that my dad used to be on the police force in Brighton?" I begin, all ready with the explanation I've prepared for her.

"Yeah?"

"I'm in a special program with Detective Hamilton," I say, which isn't untrue. "I'm sort of interning with her, and I got involved in your case." I shrug. "I guess they thought I'd be useful since we're the same age—and friends."

"Friends?"

"Well, we used to be friends. And I still consider myself your friend."

She actually smiles now, for the first time since we found her. "Thanks, I appreciate that. And that's cool, Samantha, about you being an intern with the police. I didn't know they had stuff like that in high school."

"The thing is, you can't tell anyone, okay? I mean, my internship is kind of an undercover thing, and it will mess it up if anyone else knows about it."

"Don't worry, I won't tell." Then she begins to cry again. "There's so much I will never tell..."

"It's going to be okay. Really, Kayla, I have this strong sense that God is going to bring good out of this for you."

She turns and looks at me with watery eyes. "I've been praying a lot, Samantha. I mean, really, really praying. About all I could do was pray."

"Well, God was listening. He answered your prayers."

"That's for sure," Ebony says from the front seat. "You have no idea what a miracle it is that we found you today, Kayla."

Tony nods. "Yep. It was a real honest-to-goodness miracle. And you can be thanking God that you'll probably be home for Christmas too."

"When *is* Christmas?" she asks.

"Tomorrow," I say.

"Really?" She sighs. "Is it okay if I call my mom?"

"Of course," Tony says as he pulls over to the side of the gravel road. "But that's the sheriff and emergency crew just up ahead. Let's put you into their hands first. They'll want to give you some medical treatment, and then you'll have to answer some questions and whatnot."

"And someone from my department has already called your mom," Ebony tells her. "She knows you're safe and that you'll be calling her soon."

"Oh, good."

"I asked them to call your mom too, Samantha."

"Thanks!"

And suddenly we're swarmed by medical professionals and sheriff's officials, and Kayla is swept away with barely a chance to wave a quick good-bye. I feel stunned and slightly deflated as I watch her being ushered into the back of an ambulance by a uniformed woman. Meanwhile,

Tony seems to be giving some kind of directions to one of the officers.

"Will she be okay?" I ask Ebony.

"She'll be better than she's been in weeks," Ebony says in a tired and slightly sad voice. "But it's probably going to take a fair amount of time and some good counseling before she'll *really* be okay, Samantha. And her life will certainly never be the same again."

I sigh. "Yeah, I know. But at least she's alive—and at least she's talking to God again. That's something."

"She's going to need God now more than ever."

As Tony drives us back to the hotel, I think of all that went into rescuing Kayla. All because she made one incredibly stupid decision. It kind of blows my mind.

Oh, it's not that I regret my involvement in any of this. I don't at all! And I'm so totally thankful that we found Kayla before it was too late. But it's pretty overwhelming to think of all the effort and expense that went into this search—so many people who put their lives on hold or at risk or whatever, and on Christmas Eve too...just to rescue this one girl who made one very bad decision. It makes no sense.

"There was a shepherd who had one hundred sheep..." The words of the old story, the one my dad used to tell at bedtime sometimes, begins to roll through my head. And I remember the parable that Jesus originally told—the one about the good shepherd who went to a great effort to search for one lost lamb. I remember how he left his other ninety-nine sheep behind and took off in the middle of the

night just so that he could find that one lost lamb. And I guess that's how it was with Kayla. God loves us that much!

And like that ecstatic shepherd who threw a big party after finding his beloved lamb, and just like Jesus when He rescues just one lost person, I'd have to agree that it was worth it. Totally worth it!

———

Ebony and I just took off from Phoenix, and we're on our way home. I recline my chair and close my eyes. I am so ready to just kick back for a while. The flight won't arrive in Portland for a couple of hours—perfect for a nice long snooze. It looks like Ebony has the same idea. I let out a deep sigh and feel myself slipping into a state of what I hope will be comatose slumber…

Suddenly I feel a sharp bump on my elbow and look up to see the stainless steel beverage cart attempting to move past me.

"Excuse me," says the blond flight attendant. "Your arm's in the way."

"Sorry." I pull in my arm and sit up straighter as I rub the spot where she ran into me. You'd think they'd be more careful with those carts. Anyway I'm wide-awake now. So much for my nap, although it looks like most of the passengers are fast asleep. Lucky them.

I watch the flight attendant slowly work her way up the aisle, and I can't help but think that that must be a boring job. Not only that, but a lot of the passengers, particularly during the holidays, are pretty rude and impatient.

She leans over to give a dark-haired man a cup of coffee, but as he reaches for it, the little tray is bumped and hot coffee spills all over him. He instantly leaps to his feet and attempts to brush it off, and the flight attendant apologizes and tries to help him. She finally takes him up to the front, where I assume she'll find a towel to dry him off. Poor guy, not only did he get scalded, he's probably sopping wet now too.

Then just as I think it's settled down, the man grabs the flight attendant by her arm. This is turning into one serious case of flight rage. I start to nudge Ebony in case this gets out of hand, but it looks like I'm too late. The angry man now has one arm wrapped tightly around the woman's neck, and her eyes are bulging as if she can barely breathe. But worse than that, he has a knife in his other hand! It looks like he's actually threatening to kill her. All this over a cup of coffee?

"Nobody move!" he yells with a strong accent. "I have a bomb!"

Just then I hear a scream from behind us, and I look back in time to see another man running forward in the aisle. Ebony is wide-awake now and looks just as shocked as I am. I wonder if she can help, although her gun is in her checked bag. Or maybe the man moving down the aisle is an air marshal who is armed and prepared to stop this crazy thing, but then I see that this man looks Arabic as well. And in his hand is a knife!

I'm about to stick my foot into the aisle to trip him when Ebony gives me a shove from the other side. And that's when I wake up!

"Are you okay?" asks Ebony.

I blink and look at her then look around the plane. All appears perfectly normal, and everyone is still asleep. No knives, no bombs...just peace and quiet.

"Bad dream?"

I nod and take in a deep breath. "Yeah, thank goodness. It was just a dream." Then I see the blond flight attendant up in front, and she's pouring a cup of coffee for a dark-haired guy, and suddenly I'm not sure.

Was it *just a dream*?

Discussion Guide

1. The book opens with what turns out to be a prophetic dream. What did you think when Samantha saw the news of the wreck that morning? What was your reaction to her dream?

2. Why do you think Sam wants to keep her gift a secret? What would you do in a similar situation?

3. Olivia Marsh is very supportive of Sam. Do you have someone like that in your life? Are you a friend like that? Explain.

4. Do you ever experience a "sixth sense" where you get an instinctive feeling or an intuition that later proves true?

5. Do you believe this gift of intuition comes from God? Why or why not?

6. How do you react to things that seem "supernatural"? Do you have a way to discern whether they are from God or something else? Explain.

7. Do you believe God gives special gifts to everyone, or just to those He considers special? What gifts has He given to you?

8. Why do you think God gives His children spiritual gifts? What does He want us to do with them?

9. Do you think most people live to their fullest potential, using all the gifts that God gives? Why or why not?

10. List as many gifts as you can think of.

11. Do you think that everything about God is explainable? Why or why not?

SO YOU WANT TO LEARN MORE ABOUT VISIONS AND DREAMS?

As Christians, we all have the Holy Spirit within us, and God speaks through His Spirit to guide us in our walk with Him. Most often, He speaks through our circumstances, changing our desires, giving us insight into Scripture, bringing the right words to say when speaking, or having another Christian speak words we need to hear. Yet God, in His sovereignty, may still choose to speak to us in a supernatural way, such as visions and dreams.

Our dreams, if they are truly of the Lord, should clearly line up with the Word and thus correctly reveal His character. We must always be very careful to test the words, interpretations of circumstances, dreams, visions, and advice that we receive. Satan wants to deceive us, and he has deceived many Christians into thinking that God is speaking when He is not. So how do we know if it's God's voice that we are actually hearing?

First we have to look at the Bible and see how and what He has spoken in the past, asking the question, *Does what I'm hearing line up with who God shows Himself to be and the way He works in Scripture?* Below is a list of references to dreams and visions in Scripture that will help you see what God has said about these gifts:

- Genesis is full of dreams and visions! Check out some key chapters: 15, 20, 28, 31, 37, 40, 41
- Deuteronomy 13:1–5
- Judges 7
- 1 Kings 3
- Jeremiah 23
- Several passages in the book of Daniel
- Joel 2
- The book of Ezekiel has a lot of visions
- There are a lot of dreams in the book of Matthew, specifically in chapters 1 and 2
- Acts 9, 10, 16, 18
- The whole book of Revelation

If you want to learn more and gain a balanced perspective on all this stuff, you'll probably want to research the broader category of spiritual gifts. Every Christian has at least one spiritual gift, and they are important to learn about.

Here is a list of books and websites that will help:

- *Hearing God's Voice* by Henry and Richard Blackaby
- *What's So Spiritual about Your Gifts?* by Henry and Mel Blackaby
- *Showing the Spirit* by D. A. Carson
- *The Gift of Prophecy in the New Testament and Today* by Wayne Grudem
- *Are Miraculous Gifts for Today?* by Wayne Grudem
- *Keep in Step with the Spirit* by J. I. Packer
- http://www.expository.org/spiritualgifts.htm
- www.enjoyinggodministries.com. Click on Theological Studies Section and choose Controversial Issues. Check out Session 03-04 and 18.
- www.desiringgod.org. Click on Online Library and choose Topic Index, then check out Spiritual Gifts.
  (Note: If you're doing a Google search on spiritual gifts or dreams and visions, please make sure you type in *Christian* as well. This will help you weed out a lot of deceitful stuff.)

As you continue to research and learn about spiritual gifts, always remember: The bottom line is to focus on the *Giver*, not the *gift*. God gives to us so we can glorify Him.

> "Signs and wonders are not the saving word of grace; they are God's secondary testimony to the word of his grace. Signs and wonders do not save. They are not the power of God unto salvation. They do not transform the heart—any more than music or art or drama that accompany the gospel. Signs and wonders can be imitated by Satan (2 Thessalonians 2:9; Matthew 24:24), but the gospel is utterly contrary to his nature. What changes the heart and saves the soul is the self-authenticating glory of Christ seen in the message of the gospel (2 Corinthians 3:18–4:6).
>
> But even if signs and wonders can't save the soul, they can, if God pleases, shatter the shell of disinterest; they can shatter the shell of cynicism; they can shatter the shell of false religion. Like every other good witness to the word of grace, they can help the fallen heart to fix its gaze on the gospel where the soul-saving, self-authenticating glory of the Lord shines. Therefore the early church longed for God to stretch forth his hand to heal, and that signs and wonders be done in the name of Jesus."
> —John Piper, *Desiring God*

Diary of a Teenage Girl Series

Kim

Enter Kim's World

JUST ASK, Kim book one

"Blackmailed" to regain driving privileges, Kim Peterson agrees to anonymously write a teen advice column for her dad's newspaper. No big deal, she thinks, until she sees her friends' heartaches in bold black and white. Suddenly Kim knows she does *not* have all the answers and is forced to turn to the One who does.
ISBN 1-59052-321-0

MEANT TO BE, Kim book two

Hundreds of people pray for the healing of Kim's mother. As her mother improves, Kim's relationship with Matthew develops. Natalie thinks it's wrong for a Christian to date a non-Christian, but Kim isn't so sure. However, when her mom's health goes downhill, can Kim wait to find out what's meant to be?
ISBN 1-59052-322-9

FALLING UP, Kim book three

It's summer, and Kim is overwhelmed by difficult relatives, an unpredictable boyfriend, and a best friend who just discovered she's pregnant. Kim's stress level increases until a breakdown forces her to take a vacation. How will she get through these troubling times without going crazy?
ISBN 1-59052-324-5

THAT WAS THEN..., Kim book four

Kim starts her senior year with big faith and big challenges ahead. Her best friend is pregnant and believes it's God's will that she marry the baby's father. Then Kim receives a letter from her birth mom who wants to meet her, which rocks Kim's world. Can her spiritual maturity make a difference in the lives of those around her?
ISBN 1-59052-425-X

Log onto www.DOATG.com

Chloe

Diaries Are a Girl's Best Friend

MY NAME IS CHLOE, Chloe book one

Chloe Miller, Josh's younger sister, is a free spirit with dramatic clothes and hair. She struggles with her identity, classmates, parents, boys, and whether or not God is for real. But this unconventional high school freshman definitely doesn't hold back when she meets Him in a big, personal way. Chloe expresses God's love and grace through the girl band, Redemption, that she forms, and continues to show the world she's not willing to conform to anyone else's image of who or what she should be. Except God's, that is.
ISBN 1-59052-018-1

SOLD OUT, Chloe book two

Chloe and her fellow band members must sort out their lives as they become a hit in the local community. And after a talent scout from Nashville discovers the trio, their explosive musical ministry suddenly begins to encounter conflicts with family, so-called friends, and school. Exhilarated yet frustrated, Chloe puts her dream in God's hand and prays for Him to work out the details.
ISBN 1-59052-141-2

ROAD TRIP, Chloe book three

After signing with a major record company, Redemption's dreams are coming true. Chloe, Allie, and Laura begin their concert tour with the good-looking guys in the band Iron Cross. But as soon as the glitz and glamour wear off, the girls find life on the road a little overwhelming. Even rock-solid Laura appears to be feeling the stress—and Chloe isn't quite sure how to confront her about the growing signs of drug addiction...
ISBN 1-59052-142-0

FACE THE MUSIC, Chloe book four

Redemption has made it to the bestseller chart, but what Chloe and the girls need most is some downtime to sift through the usual high school stress with grades, friends, guys, and the prom. Chloe struggles to recover from a serious crush on the band leader of Iron Cross. Then just as an unexpected romance catches Redemption by surprise, Caitlin O'Conner—whose relationship with Josh is taking on a new dimension—joins the tour as a chaperone. Chloe's wild ride only speeds up, and this one-of-a-kind musician faces the fact that life may never be normal again.
ISBN 1-59052-241-9

Log onto www.DOATG.com